The Girl with a Baby

Sylvia Olsen

sononis
PRESS
WINLAW, BRITISH COLUMBIA

NATIONAL LIBRARY OF CANADA CATALOGUING IN PUBLICATION DATA

Olsen, Sylvia, 1955-
     The girl with a baby / Sylvia Olsen.

ISBN 1-55039-142-9

     1. Teenage pregnancy—Juvenile fiction. 2. Indian teenagers—Juvenile
fiction. 3. Teenage mothers—Juvenile fiction. I. Title.

PS8579.L728G57 2003   jC813'.6   C2003-905592-2

Sono Nis Press most gratefully acknowledges the support for our publishing program
provided by the Government of Canada through the Book Publishing Industry
Development Program (BPIDP), The Canada Council for the Arts, and the British
Columbia Arts Council.

Edited by Laura Peetoom
Copy edited by Audrey McClellan
Cover and interior design by Jim Brennan

Published by
SONO NIS PRESS
Box 160
Winlaw, BC V0G 2J0
1-800-370-5228

sononis@netidea.com
www.sononis.com

Printed and bound in Canada by
Houghton Boston Printers

Distributed in the U.S. by
Orca Book Publishers
Box 468
Custer, WA 98240-0468
1-800-210-5277

The Canada Council | Le Conseil des Arts
for the Arts | du Canada

For Heather and Yetsa

1

I dreaded giving birth since I first realized I was pregnant. I dreaded it so much that I succeeded in denying it would ever happen. The dread got squashed into a thin line under a thick layer of Don't Think About It. When it finally did happen I wished I had thought about it, but then, what good would it have done? I would still be standing here in total pain, nothing around except fear, freaking out, and trying to stay in control.

I sucked in a raggy breath and cried, "Where's Teh? Joey has to find her."

I held onto Pete and dug my fingers into his palms. The blood was drained from the skin that stretched over my knuckles, and my nails were sickly white.

Hurry up, Teh.

"She'll be here. I think she went to town to get her hair done," Pete said.

I tried to stand up and straighten my back, but my belly weighed it down. I rested my head and arms across the hospital bed and leaned against Pete's arm and shoulder.

The doctor stood up and brushed her arm against the side of her face to sweep a lone strand of hair out of her eyes. Her head was covered with a blue cap, tightly gathered around her face with white elastic. She smiled and placed her hand gently on my shoulder.

Pain—like a trailer truck, barreling down the street behind me, gaining momentum by the second—smacked into me. Ran over me. Then, like a giant vise, it sank its teeth into my belly. It held on and turned slowly, twisting and contorting my insides.

Instinct made me breathe. There was nothing I could do about it. If only I could stop breathing I could put an end to the whole thing. I could back out, black out. I tightened my lips and filled my cheeks with air until they stung.

"Concentrate, Jane," the doctor said. Her voice sliced through the pain noise that was buzzing in my ears like a swarm of bees. "You're doing fine. Quick breaths. Try not to hold on."

Gradually the monster released its grip. Starting from my fingertips and toes and edging toward my belly I loosened up, bit by bit.

"Pete. Thanks for being here, big brother," I sputtered as soon as the pain let go of my tongue.

I examined my oldest brother's features. Small beads of sweat clustered on his broad square forehead and trickled down his thick jaw, pooling around the black hairs on his chin. His bloodshot eyes were yellow green under the strange hospital lights.

"I'm trying, Jane," Pete said. "But I'm not much good with girl stuff."

I said, "Just hang in there with me until Teh gets here."

Time was elastic. It stretched tight into what seemed like forever and then sprang back too soon between contractions. Gradually at first, and then quickly, another pain surged through my body. This time it started in my lower back and deep between my legs.

Please, Teh, hurry. I'm so scared.

The doctor stood close to me. Her voice was loud and low. "Short little puffs. Concentrate, Jane."

I tightened my grip on Pete's hand. I took a short gasp. And then another. The contraction grabbed every body part and knotted them together. It held the ends and pulled. Tight. Tighter.

I can't do this anymore.

My mind was getting slippery. It flowed, greasy, outside myself. I looked back.

A teenage girl leans forward against a hospital bed, legs apart. A threadbare, blue gray, institution nightgown hangs in front of her body, tied in a bow at the neck, exposing her bra strap and her bare butt and legs. Her stringy hair is stuck in clumps to her sweaty forehead, back, and cheeks. A doctor sits on a stool between the girl's legs. She looks up, her hands press on the girl's stomach.

Hammering pain, relentless.

Finally the pain faded. It backed away from my arms and legs and then my belly, like it did the other times. As each pain left I was weaker, watery. My bones and blood vessels floated in a quivery mass.

Pete whispered, "You're strong, Jane. I have to tell you."

I spread my legs a little to ease the pressure on my knees. My feet felt thick, like cement blocks, and numb from the cold floor. Panic crept around me like a wildcat, nipping and clawing. I scratched back. I was performing a high-wire balancing act between being in control and hysterical.

It wasn't only the pain. It was Teh. Where was she? Then a familiar voice interrupted my fear.

"Where is she? Is the baby coming now? Do we know how far along she is?"

I heard Teh's voice first and then her steps. Tears welled up inside me.

Teh! Teh! I hurt, Teh. I hurt so bad.

I wanted to collapse into Teh's arms. Give my pain over to her. But she couldn't make it go away. I knew that.

A man dressed in a white coat and a nurse followed her into the room. A space between the pains gave me a chance to listen.

"I'm Dr. Lawrence, a pediatrician," the man said. He reached out and shook Teh's hand. "I've been called in in case there's a problem when the baby arrives."

Teh lowered one eye as if to focus. It was Teh's way of getting a better grip on a situation. "Is the baby okay?" she asked.

"We don't have any reason to believe otherwise. But we don't know what we're dealing with—not even if the baby's early, late, or on time. She hasn't been to a doctor once throughout her pregnancy . . ."

"I know that," Teh butted into the doctor's words. She wasn't one to be told what she already knew. She shifted her body weight from one leg to the other. Her silver-streaked black hair was bunched in a heavy knot and clipped with beads and feathers. Second-hand Annie, she called herself. Loose harem pants, discards from the 70s, flowed under an orange-and-black patterned cape and rumpled over her running shoes, the only thing she bought new.

"We didn't have time to do any tests," the nurse said.

Teh hesitated and then said, "Well, it looks like the baby thinks it's time to come into this world." She turned toward me and I saw her eyes soften. The creases between her eyebrows flattened out.

"It's time," she said quietly, nodding her head. "It's time."

She walked over to the bed and wrapped her arms around me. She was firm and soft and I breathed in her lavender and myrrh body oils. Teh held onto me while another contraction came and went.

"You okay, girl?" she asked.

"Now *you're* here."

"Baby Jane, I'd'a been here earlier if I'd known. But here's me thinking I have time to get my hair done. I was telling Cory at the salon that my baby granddaughter is going to have herself a baby ..."

Teh's voice was like a pressure gauge. It wasn't how loud she spoke, or how deep. It had more to do with steadiness, the steadiness I had in my stomach when I listened to her. I swayed my hips back and forth. The sound of her voice was safe, like a warm house and hot milk.

"Kate's with Joey," Teh was saying. "They've taken off again to look for your father. Joey said he's going to try and pick up Trevor, too. Does Trevor even know he's going to be a father this evening?"

"No." Fortunately Pete answered for me. I was fuzzy. Coming and going. "Trevor doesn't know yet. We didn't have time to tell anyone except Joey. Jane and I went to the doctor's office. The doctor said she needed some tests to find out how pregnant Jane was. By the time we got home, Jane said her back hurt. I didn't know what the hell to do so Joey and I brought her in here to Emergency. A doctor looked at her and said she was five centimetres dilated, whatever that means, and they rushed her down here to the maternity ward. I've been with her ever since."

"Teh! Teh!" I cried. "There's another pain, only worse. I can't do this. I've never had a baby before."

"There's a first time for everyone. There are so many things we should have talked about. And here we are, in the middle of it."

"Okay, Jane," Dr. Carlson interrupted. "You're going into transition now. Listen to me closely . . . "

I stared at the doctor. Through the buzz of the pain her words found their way directly to my brain.

"Uh-huh," I mumbled.

I was crystal clear in spite of the jumble of pain and hospital noise.

"Jane," the doctor continued, "listen to your body and let it tell you what it needs to do."

My legs shook so bad I could barely stand up. Lying down hurt too much and I couldn't sit. So I sprawled my arms and shoulders across the bed to get the weight off my legs a little.

It's not one thing or another. It's confusion and clarity; it's brutal agony and then bliss between contractions. I don't know one thing about birthing a baby, but I know what to do and I do it. I'm hanging on a ledge ready to fling myself over into the crazies and I'm swaying my hips from side to side, keeping time with the pulse of nature. I'm gutsy bloody stinging sweaty screaming lusty nature, resting and waiting for the next moment. And I'm doing it.

Another pain came and went.

Teh leaned over and laid her head beside mine. For a few moments we shared the same stale hospital air.

"Jane. You all right?" she asked.

"Yeah. My body seems to know what to do." My words stretched across time. Each moment was preparing for the next.

"You two listen up." Teh raised her voice so Pete could hear. "Right now Jane's part of something bigger than all of us. She's part of a long line of great mothers. Your mother, your grandmothers and aunties on both your dad's and mom's

10

side for many generations are strong women and mothers. So are the women in our spirit world. Jane has their power in her body and in her spirit."

A loose curl bobbed up and down against Teh's cheek as she spoke. I wanted to reach out and tuck it behind her ear, but it nodded at me. I couldn't see the aunties, grandmothers, and spirit women and I didn't understand all of Teh's words, but they were like fresh sheets pulled snug around the corners of the mattress and tucked in. For a second everything made sense.

Teh stroked my greasy hair. She pulled it back and twisted it around her fingers into a knot.

"I wish Dad would get here," I said.

"Joey and Kate will find him soon."

"I wish Mom was here." Tears filled the corners of my eyes.

"She is," Teh said.

Mom. Mom?

Another pain suddenly exploded. This time it started in my heart and then spilled over and seeped through my body. Pete hooked onto my arm on one side and Teh hooked under the other.

I became a vortex, the drain, sucking down water and suds, bits of dirt and grease. Swirling the smells, sounds, and images around, around, around.

A doctor sits on a footstool between my legs.

Close your legs. Put on some underwear. What is she looking at? Pete's Toronto cap.

You look stoned, brother. Are you drunk? You smell helpful, like fried bread.

Teh's skin is soft. It rubs up against mine. A spring is loose.

I smell clams and lavender and myrrh. And hear old people.

11

I hurt. I really hurt.

Low streams of warm yellow evening sun shine in the window.
Mom, Mom?

Mom's frail body lies propped up in a stack of pillows. Saucer-sized black eyes gaze from holes set deep in her protruding forehead.
Her skin is ghostly white. She smiles a strained, pale-lips-stretched-over-teeth sort of smile. Her bony fingers draw figures over my
child-pudgy hands.

"Jane, I'm leaving this sick body, sweet girl. I'm going away.
But I'll never leave you. I'll love you from wherever I am. Teh
will take my place. You help her take care of your brothers and
father. You be the most you can be. Remember, I'll always be
there for you, Sweet Baby Jane."

The pain dissolved Mom's words as it backed away. My
nose, my mouth, my eyes were streaming. Pete patted my face
with a cloth.

Pains lasted longer and came closer together. Spaces
between contractions were only moments. Images bolted in
and out of time and lingered in hazy places.

A young girl, a kid leans over a hospital bed.

Five years old. Drenched long black hair—tousled—over her
eyes, shoulders, and down to the dip in her back. Freshly mown
grass tickles her feet. She giggles and skips through the sprinkler.
Her older brother laughs as she flits back and forth. She reaches
down and pulls off her wet shorts.

"You're too old for that, Baby Jane. You go inside to change."
Cover your butt.

A warm stream of water trickled down my legs.

Where's the cool face cloth, Pete? My tears are trickling down
my inner thighs. God, wipe my nose. It's running down my legs.

"What's that? What's going on?" Pete exclaimed. He
jumped aside.

"It's okay," the doctor explained. "That's just her water. The amniotic fluid the baby was in ... "

Suddenly the warm fluid gushed from between my legs and puddled under my feet.

The water's okay.

The hospital terry cloth slippers slopped up the liquid.

Mom? Mom? Where are you? The sprinkler is warm. What did I do with my shorts?

The doctor's words were soupy, stirred.

Okay, it's okay. Don't worry, Jane.

Her strong steady voice reassured me.

And Teh. And Pete. I'm not afraid.

Pain filled every space, every moment. It filled the tiny places in my body, the in-between bits I didn't know I had.

There is no room left, not even for air.

I had come to the end of the road.

Then something I didn't recognize came from a place I had never been. Suddenly my legs were stone cold and shook out of control.

"I think we better lift her up onto the bed," Teh alerted the doctor.

"Okay, Jane?" the doctor asked.

Do what you have to.

My lips could no longer form words. Teh and Pete lifted my shoulders and back while the doctor hefted my butt up. My legs flopped, spastic, like chickens that had had their heads cut off. It was my body, but it wasn't connected to my brain in any way that I recognized.

Suddenly I had an overwhelming urge to push. I clenched my teeth, grabbed Pete's hand, and drove my hips into the bed.

"Good push, Jane. You're doing great ... " The doctor's words blurred.

My belly had never looked so big. I couldn't imagine that one push or a million pushes could make something that big come out of my body.

"Uuuurrrrrgggg . . . " Unfamiliar sounds spewed out of my gut.

"Push again," the doctor urged. "Slow and steady."

Pain was replaced by formidable determination. The thing inside me was coming out. I was going to push it out if it was the last thing I did in my life. All the fiery, watery, earthy, stormy forces inside me were roped together, harnessed and pulling, pushing together.

I bit down on my lip, squeezed my eyes shut, and pushed hard.

Loud guttural noises erupted, followed by another long, caveman grunt. The baby was holding onto my guts, and it felt like if I pushed any harder it would pull me inside out.

I heard a pop. Or felt it. Like a cork. And then the most amazing relief, release. A gush of warm fluid swam under my butt and thighs.

"It's the head!" I heard Teh cry.

The next push brought with it what felt like the biggest bowel movement in history. I was hot and wet and drifting through time and space.

Fingers of warm gold light massage my skin.

"It's a girl!"

My mind found its way back into the room in time to see the doctor place the small baby into Teh's hands.

"Jane, meet your new baby girl." Teh held out the tiny baby as if she was holding her up to the gods.

I reached up and our hands met as we both lowered the scrawny bundle of purple arms and legs onto my chest. It didn't weigh much more than a soccer ball or a school binder. I was relieved when I counted ten toes and ten fingers. Her face was creased and red, like an old tomato. Her skin looked like crinkled cellophane, and her eyes were stuck tight shut with white goo. She looked human, but barely—she could have been a creature from another world.

Pete peered over my shoulder. I could tell he was thinking the same kind of stuff I was.

"She's my baby, Teh!" I cried. "This is for real, Pete. She's my baby."

Tears ran off my chin and onto her blanket. "Baby, meet your Uncle Pete. Baby, meet your Great-Grandma Teh."

Pete pulled his finger up to his niece's tiny face. He traced his finger over her body, making figures in the air. A chill ran up my spine.

"Outrageous, Jane. Fucking amazing. Hardcore, man," Pete said. "I'm freaking, little sister."

Out of nowhere I had an enormous cramp in my stomach. *God, not again. Please, no more pain.*

Then I recognized an old familiar feeling.

"Teh," I called. "I'm starving. Can Pete order a pizza?"

"Yeah. Good idea." Pete perked up. "I'll get it delivered."

Teh tossed Pete a roll of money just as Joey, Kate, Trevor, and Dad walked into the room.

"Hey, am I ever glad you guys made it. Meet Destiny, my baby girl."

2

A loud buzzing noise woke me up. I couldn't tell where it was coming from and I didn't know where I was. The room was pitch-black except for a thin line of pale yellow light from a door at the end of the bed, which was open a bit. I cupped my hands over my ears and shook my head to stop the ringing. When I heard the plastic hospital pillow crinkle, I remembered.

My neck was sweaty, strings of hair were wrapped around my forehead, and the ties of my nightie almost choked me. I wanted to sit up, untwist myself, and get loose, but my body felt like a lump of wet clay—my arms and legs were as heavy as waterlogged cedar posts.

I lay in the dark and placed my hand on my belly. It wasn't tight and round anymore. It was soft and squishy like jelly. My fingers sank into the folds of my mushy skin. Suddenly out of my groggy half-sleep I had a mind seizure.

Where's my baby? What happened to my baby?

I felt like I had swallowed a boulder and it sank to the pit of my stomach. I grabbed my head with both hands, shook it to clear my mind, and gulped for air. I held onto the edge of the bed and hunched up on my elbow into a half-sitting position.

Wake up, Jane. Think about it. Your baby isn't in your stomach anymore. You're in the hospital. You've already had your baby. And she's—god, where is she?

My mind fought the fuzziness, the half-awake nightmare. I squinted to set the light straight so I could see around the inky room. Murky shadows outlined two bulky armchairs and a small round table covered with a pile of neatly stacked clothes. The thick musty smell of hospital bodies and industrial cleansers stuck in the back of my throat.

Where's my baby?

Panic swelled in my gut.

I dragged myself up to a full sitting position. My heart was pounding so hard it drowned out the vibrating hum. All I could hear was blood rushing behind my ears.

Think about it, Jane. Where did you put your baby? Who took your baby?

When my mind started to clear I remembered a nurse coming into the room after everyone had left the night before. We had finished the pizzas and then Dad, Pete, Joey, Kate, Teh, and Trevor lined up next to my bed. One by one they threw their arms around me, kissed me, and said their goodbyes and their we-can't-believe-you-had-a-baby, you-shocked-the-hell-out-of-us-Janes. Trevor had been the last one out.

He said, "Goodbye, Jane, I'll see you soon." I thought he was going to leave. But he turned back into the room and said, "You did really good, Jane. You're tough shit, girl. I'd'a been freaking out if it was me, man."

I remembered looking at him and thinking, god, he doesn't sound like a father. He didn't look much like a father either. His baggy skater pants were hooked on his hips and bunching over his grubby running shoes. It was long after nine o'clock in the evening when everyone said goodbye, but he still wore his sunglasses.

You got that right, you'd'a been freaking out.

Still Trevor had hung around, as if he wanted to say something or do something. He nodded his head and rocked from his heels to the balls of his feet. He held one hand on the door and the other in a bent-finger wave.

"Yeah?" I said.

"Bye, Jane."

"Bye."

What was that about?

Anyway, when he had finally closed the door, it opened almost immediately.

"How are you, Jane? I'm Cindy, your nurse tonight." The cheery woman popped the thermometer in my mouth and then wrapped a strap around my arm.

"Just have to get your temperature and blood pressure and then I'll leave you alone," she said.

Once she had checked the instruments, she tucked them next to the baby and said, "Everything looks fine to me. We'll take your baby down to the nursery tonight, if you want. You'll get a better night's sleep."

I remembered watching the nurse push my baby's bed-on-wheels out the door. I remembered hearing it rattle down the hall. Come to think about it, I didn't remember turning out the light or lying down or pulling my covers over my shoulders. But I remembered falling like a wheelbarrow full of wet cement into such a deep sleep it almost hurt.

The nurse took her. She's fine. She's in the nursery so I can sleep.

But I was wide awake. I pulled the sheets back, uncovered my body, and stared at the gray outline of my legs. It was a good thing that the room was so dark and I could see only the faded lines of my lumpy shape under the rumpled hospital gown. It made me think of last summer when Allison and I went to Wal-Mart to try on shoes.

"Here, try these!" Allison had laughed when she threw me a pair of black fake-patent-leather heels. They were the kind ladies with big hair, leopard skin skirts, and over-the-shoulder tank tops wear to the bar. I kicked off my worn-out running shoes and pushed my feet into the flimsy shoes. I stood up and wobbled over to the mirror and looked at my feet.

"Allison, you gotta come and take a look at these feet," I had cried. "They look like they belong to someone else."

The shoes didn't look bad. It was the feet. They didn't look like they were mine. They looked like they should be attached to another pair of legs.

Now my body felt the same way. It looked like it belonged to one of the women dressed in pastel sweatpants and baggy oversized floral shirts we saw shopping at Wal-Mart. I thought I would feel light and small after I gave birth. Instead I felt like a great big mountain of fat. Only loose and shifty.

Nothing seemed to want to move on its own, so I lifted my hands and pushed my legs over the side of the bed and then fished around with my toes until I found the blue terry cloth slippers. I stuffed my feet in. I picked up the hospital gown that was lying at the end of the bed and slipped it on like a housecoat.

"It's your body," I told myself. "You better get used to it."

I knew it wouldn't be easy. I remembered playing basketball in gym class only about four months before. I was almost the shortest one in the class, but I was one of the best checks on the court. And the day Mr. Goodacre had challenged the gym class to see who could walk on their hands.

No one could take one step except me. I had walked ten steps in the air. No one could believe it.

How surprised they will be when they find out I was five months pregnant.

Now *that* body had turned into *this* body. My legs and feet, like pendulums with heavy weights attached, swung back and forth over the side of the hospital bed. I remembered before I got pregnant buying size three jeans, even though they were a little baggy in the waist, and spandex workout shorts and a short black sweater that barely touched my jeans. It had left a thin slice of my flat belly exposed and showed off my emerald belly-button ring. As I looked at myself now, it all seemed like some other life.

By the time I was four or five months pregnant, I started to notice my belly protruding out the front, and my waist thickening around the sides and back. I still played basketball, danced, and did gymnastics, but every morning I had to think of a way to cover up. I had worn baggy T-shirts and sweatshirts and Joey or Pete's old sweatpants. Every day I noticed something change. My arms thickened. My butt flattened out across the back and my hips spread around the sides. The worst thing was that my face looked like it did when I was four years old, with a double chin and chubby cheeks. Once in a while I caught a glimpse of my profile in a mirror. I pulled my T-shirt tight to show my bulging middle. For some reason it grew flat and wide. It never poked straight out the front unless I was lying on my back. Which I made sure I never did if anyone was around.

The bigger I got the wider I got. As the months passed by, every day I expected someone to walk up to me at school in the hall and say, "Hey, Jane. You're pregnant. We've all known forever." How could they not know?

I thought for sure Allison would figure it out. I wished she would. Once Corrine had asked me if it bothered me.

"What?" I asked, thinking, *Here it comes*, and feeling nervous and relieved both.

"Putting on weight," she said. "Doesn't it make you feel gross?"

"No, not really," I said. She didn't ask why or how.

The amazing thing, the thing I still couldn't believe, was that Teh hadn't guessed. Teh was usually the first person to know things about people. And she didn't often need to be told. She knew almost the day Aunt Lily got pregnant with Lori Jean, and she knew that Uncle Danny wasn't the father. Tommy George was. She knew when Dad lost his job. He had left the house every morning at 7 a.m. with his lunch packed, and returned at 4:30. Until one day when he was stepping out the front door and Teh had called out to him, "Sooner you admit you got fired, sooner you'll get yourself another job." Teh knew Mom had breast cancer before she went to the doctor. And she knew that neither the doctor nor anybody else was going to be able to do anything about it. But except for her dream, Teh didn't suspect a thing about me. "Don't bug her. Young girls all put on a little weight," she explained to Pete or Joey one morning when they called me Chubby Cheeks. "It's part of becoming a woman."

Now I lifted my lunky body off the hospital bed and shuffled out the door. My legs were so wobbly I had to hold onto the handrail to keep from collapsing on the floor. The hall was deserted. No one sat at the nurse's station outside my room. I couldn't hear any babies crying or nurses talking, nothing. Nightlights cast willowy shadows on the walls of the dark, silent, deserted hall. Only one bright light shone from a window down at the other end.

Shulft, shulft, shulft. I dragged my slippers along the floor. When I reached the lighted window I stood and peered in. Two rows of bassinets lined the walls of the small room. Nurse Cindy sat in a rocking chair, feeding a tiny baby. I looked from one bassinet to the next, trying to find my baby, and then tapped on the window. The nurse looked up and then opened the door.

"What are you doing here?" She looked surprised. "It's after 2 a.m. You should be sleeping."

"I woke up and got worried about my baby," I said, peering anxiously until I finally found the bassinet that said *Williams, Jane. Baby girl.*

"Destiny," I said.

"What did you say?"

"Destiny," I repeated. "See here?" I pointed to the little baby sleeping soundly. "The Williams baby girl. She's mine. Her name is Destiny."

"That's a beautiful name. Did you choose it?"

"Yes."

"Why?"

"Because I like the sound of it. I read what it means in the dictionary and I like the meaning."

"What does it mean?"

"It means what's going to happen no matter what you do—but it's also power—the power that decides what your life's going to be like. I think my baby has the power to make my life. It seems like no matter what I had wished and hoped for myself, she's here. She must be my destiny. She's already changed everything."

"Does she have a middle name?"

"Mae. Her name is Destiny Mae Williams. Can I pick her up and hold her?"

"Of course you can. Pull up that rocking chair and sit down. But are you sure you don't want to go back to bed?"

"Yeah, I'm sure."

I plunked myself into the rocking chair. I lifted my tiny baby up to my face and inhaled a long, intoxicating breath. It felt like I was sucking the last drops of a delicious strawberry milkshake through a straw. I didn't move until I felt Destiny's delicate in-and-out breath against my cheek.

"Ummm. She smells so pure and fresh."

I snuggled close to my baby. I didn't want to lose that awesome smell of her being brand new. I had the same kind of feeling I got when I opened a new box of running shoes or sat in a new car or first dressed a new Barbie doll.

I whispered, "You're Destiny because you've changed my life. You're Mae because you had the most beautiful grandmother who will never get to meet you or hold you. You have her name, baby girl, so she will live forever in you. And you're a Williams because you're mine."

It felt like I was meeting someone I had known forever but had never looked at real close. Her face was smooth now, and her skin soft as velvet. She wasn't tomato red anymore but milk-chocolate brown. She was perfectly beautiful. I recognized her eyes even though they were closed. They were large surface ovals, not round circles like mine, or thin slits like Dad's, or deep-set-in like Teh's. They were arched and then tapered, almost turned up in the corners, just like Trevor's eyes. Her nose had a strong bridge and delicate nostrils, although it was hard to tell since it was flattened out from the birthing on one side and swollen on the other. I worried about that and hoped it wouldn't stay smudged up for too long.

"Her name is Destiny Mae Williams," I said. "But she looks kind of like her father. She has his eyes."

"She's beautiful," Cindy said. The nurse watched me closely. She looked like she was worried that I was going to drop my baby or something. "You must feel proud."

Proud? I thought about it for a moment. Proud of what? Proud of getting pregnant and not telling anyone? Proud of having a baby at fourteen? Proud of disappointing Teh and Dad and Joey and Pete and everyone else? Proud of hurting my friends? Proud of shocking my teachers? No, proud wasn't something I had felt much lately. And yet . . .

"Proud." I got my tongue tied around the word. Then I looked down at the peaceful little baby girl tucked in my arms. "I guess I am proud."

"It must be hard, after what you've been through. How does it feel now you've had your baby?"

How do I feel?

Tears stung my eyelids. The walls I had built around me and my secret, walls I had so carefully set up to keep me in and everyone else out, were starting to shake.

I had been living a lie for so long, and everyone had believed me. But now my lie was out. Literally. If I had murdered someone or robbed a bank, if I had disguised myself as a boy or pretended to be rich, I might have had a chance, maybe just a slim chance, but a chance at least, of never being caught. I could have built one lie on the next and maybe even would have believed my own lie. It happens. I've read about people who do it. But my lie wasn't like that. My lie was like setting the clock on a time bomb and then pretending you hadn't. You just can't fake being not pregnant when you are.

How do I feel?

The walls were beginning to crumble around me. I wanted to talk, but the words stacked up on top of each other. There was a traffic jam in my mind and it backed up in my throat. I hadn't talked to anyone about anything. Except for Trevor, and all he had wanted to talk about was how to get an abortion.

"No way," I had said. And I stuck to it. Once I was five months pregnant, he realized it was too late. Then Trevor stopped talking to me even about being pregnant. I didn't talk to myself much about it either, except to decide how to hide it, what to wear, and what to say so no one would find out.

How do I feel?

I hadn't seen it coming. I didn't expect one simple question to let loose the pain I had packed so tightly in my chest. I didn't know that I hurt. Not until that moment. I tried to talk but I swallowed instead. I gulped back painful lumps in my throat.

Breathe in deeply and then exhale the pain. Let it go.

Nurse Cindy passed me a box of tissue. I wiped my eyes and nose. Silently we rocked the babies while I fought for control.

Each time I swallowed it felt like I was filling my stomach with stones. They gurgled and tossed until I retched. I turned my head to avoid throwing up all over Destiny. Then instead of puke, words spewed out of my mouth.

"I think I feel more scared than proud. And I'm pretty embarrassed too. It's kind of too much. I don't know what I'm going to do. And I feel tired and beat-up inside. My body's wrecked. I feel like I have been living a lie for so long, not telling anyone I was pregnant—until yesterday. Mostly I feel like I let everyone down. Everyone had so much faith in me."

My chest heaved like silent rolling waves, with each breath reaching and releasing. Tears streamed to the tip of my chin and dropped onto the faded pink blanket wrapped tightly around Destiny. Relief came over me. I let go of the words I had kept locked up for so long. I couldn't stop them now I'd started.

"Did you know that Teh and my dad and my brothers and nobody at school or anyone in the whole world except Trevor knew I was pregnant? Not even my very best friends. And Trevor just wanted me to have an abortion. He got all mad at me and then wouldn't talk about it anymore."

Nurse Cindy sat silently rocking the baby. She didn't stare or gasp. "They told me a little bit about you when I came on shift tonight. I have heard stories like yours before, but I have never met someone who was able to keep her pregnancy hidden right up to delivery. How did you do it?" she asked.

"I didn't mean to keep it a secret at first. I wanted to tell somebody. I wanted to tell Allison, she's my best friend. And Teh, she's my grandmother. But I couldn't say the words. They got caught in my throat and wouldn't come out. I tried a few times—to tell Teh—but my voice was silent. One day Teh said she had a dream that I was pregnant and she was sure the dream was true. When she asked me, I said, 'No, of course not, Teh. I'm not pregnant.' And then from that day on I couldn't go back on my word. My whole life became my secret."

"Didn't anyone suspect anything?"

"I wore big sweatshirts. And no one would suspect anything of me. I'm the good Williams. I'm the *only* good Williams. I get good grades, I volunteer at the animal shelter, I'm in the drama club at school. I'm such a good girl no one would suspect anything of me. At least they never used to before today."

The nursery was quiet except for the vibrating hum, which seemed to be everywhere in the hospital, and the *creak, creak* of the rocking chairs.

"I never thought in a million years that I would be a

mother at fourteen. Did you know I'm only fourteen?"

"They told me that too when I came in to work. And they told me you did an amazing job of birthing your daughter. They said they had never seen a birthing like it."

"I didn't know anything about birthing. I hadn't gone to the doctor or anything. But when it came to doing it, somehow I knew what to do. Teh told me to dig deep into my past and the strong women in my family would help me out. I could feel some of them."

"You must be tired." Cindy stood up and placed the baby into his bassinet.

"It would have been better if I'd prepared a little bit. I was pretty stupid, wasn't I?"

"I don't think you're stupid at all, Jane. I think you're very brave."

Brave? That was another thing I hadn't thought about me. Scared out of my mind, more like it. Not brave. But I would sure need to be brave from now on.

"The doctor was awesome," I said. "That lady doctor. She told me what was happening and what to do. I don't know what I would have done without her."

"You are really lucky she was available."

"I'm pretty lucky all the way around," I said, although lucky didn't seem to fit how I felt either. I had to tell myself the lucky things, even if I didn't feel them. "I'm lucky it all turned out so well. I'm lucky Destiny is healthy even though I didn't go to the doctor or anything. And I'm lucky I got such a good family. Think of all the things that could have gone wrong if I hadn't been so lucky. It's not as if I planned anything out."

Cindy picked up another baby and began to change the diaper.

"I'm lucky you were here tonight to talk to me." I placed Destiny back into her bed. "Thank you. I don't feel as scared anymore."

"Destiny Mae Williams will be just fine here with me tonight," Cindy said. "Now you go back to your room and get some sleep. Do you need a sleeping pill?"

"No. I'll be okay. Thank you," I said again.

Shulft, shulft, shulft. My slippers sounded a little lighter as I shuffled back to my room. I left a lot of stuff in the nursery with Cindy.

3

"Hey, Jane!"

Allison and Corrine woke me up, dopey from a hot afternoon sleep. The three of us had been inseparable since kindergarten. For me, it was Allison and me and then Corrine was always there. But since I started to get really pregnant, it was me on the outside of the threesome.

I rolled over.

"Hey, guys," I said, still hazy.

Allison entered the room first and sat next to me on the bed. Corrine stood back against the door.

"Here," Allison said and handed me a bright yellow stuffed bunny. "Congratulations."

"Yeah, here." Corrine tossed a bouquet of orange and yellow lilies onto the bed.

"Thanks."

I played self-consciously with the floppy bunny ears and glanced at my friends as they shifted uncomfortably.

"Thanks, you guys," I said. The words hung in the air.

"Hey, come here," Allison said. She pulled me toward

her and swung her arms around me. Tears spurted everywhere as she buried her head in my neck.

"I am so shocked, Jane. Why didn't you tell me? I can't believe you didn't tell me," she sputtered. "You had a *baby*. I'm your *best friend*."

Why didn't you guess? I asked her silently. From the day I realized I missed my period for the third month in a row I wanted to tell her.

Allison, I'm pregnant.

The words wouldn't come. For some reason I couldn't get my lips around them. Each day I didn't say them made it harder the next day.

Then came the day I noticed a squiggle. My stomach felt jumpy. I placed my hand over my belly and something blipped inside. I thought I was imagining it so I pressed my hand deeper and the same thing happened again.

I had lain on my bed, unable to move my arms and legs. The room got fuzzy and shifty and I thought I was going to puke. When I finally sat up, all I wanted to do was phone Allison. I wanted to run over to her house and collapse on her lap. I was terrified. I wanted Allison to feel the thing growing in my stomach. I wanted to tell her what a jerk Trevor was being. But now I was worried that Allison would say, "Why didn't you tell me earlier?" So I kept my lips sealed.

It felt good to be close to her again. We hung onto each other as Allison sobbed. But it was different. Something had changed. I knew it and I could tell she did too. We were both remembering our promise. The promise I had broken.

We had made the promise the day Allison ran from behind the school, where it had happened, all the way to my house without stopping. She pounded breathlessly at the door until I finally answered, and she flopped into my arms.

"He kissed me. Aaron Medley kissed me. Right on my mouth. A full mouth kiss. He opened his mouth and pressed his tongue against my lips and my tongue. Tongue to tongue," she babbled.

"How was it? Did you like it?"

"I don't know." She began to calm down. "It was kind of drippy. And he kept pushing his tongue against my teeth. But he kissed me, Jane, he kissed me."

That day we made the promise. "We promise always and forever to tell each other everything. Our deepest secrets. No boy will ever come between us."

"I promise." Allison held her hand up high in the air.

"I promise." I high-fived her.

"Promise. Promise. Promise," we called out together, slapping each other's hands each time.

And I did tell her everything. Except that I was pregnant.

I should have told her about the sex, but the way it happened it wasn't something I wanted to tell anyone. I hadn't planned on it and I didn't even see it coming. It was after school and Trevor and I were in the family room. I was sitting on the recliner on his lap while we were watching *All in the Family* reruns. He kissed my neck and stroked my shoulder. Gradually his hand moved down the front of my chest and under my T-shirt. It slipped lower and lower until he was rubbing my breasts. In one way it didn't feel that good because he was kind of rough, and every once in a while I flinched from pain, but in another way it seemed daring, and I wasn't daring very often.

I felt his thing sticking into my thigh. The more he rubbed my breasts, the harder it got. I wasn't thinking about what I was doing when I shifted my butt and stuck my hand down between his legs and rubbed his jeans right on the bulge. He froze for a couple of seconds, stopped rubbing my breasts, and then started to shake. I stopped.

"God, Jane," he said, "you can't just do that and then quit. I'm burning up." He pushed me onto the floor. "When guys get like this they gotta do it." He was panting and grabbing himself while he tried to undress me. His hands were sticky with sweat and he fumbled around as if he had two left hands. I just lay there as if it was happening to someone else. He tugged my boot off and unzipped my jeans. He pulled one of my legs free from my pants. Then he unzipped his jeans and pushed them and his boxers down to his ankles. It wasn't until that moment that I realized it was really going to happen. He started pushing his thing into me.

"What about a condom?" I asked. "We can't do it without a condom." If he heard me, he ignored what I said and carried on.

"Trevor," I said. "Stop!" I struggled a little but I didn't want to hurt his feelings.

A condom. We gotta find a condom.

I thought if I could get up, I would look in the boys' room. Maybe Joey had one in his dresser. Or maybe I could look in the downstairs bathroom medicine cabinet—I remembered seeing a box there with a woman and man on the front and an ocean scene behind them with palm trees and volcanoes.

Less than half a minute passed, and Trevor crawled off me and pulled his pants up from around his ankles. I watched him stuff his thing inside his boxers and zip up his jeans.

"I gotta go, Jane. See you," he said as he slipped on his running shoes without untying or tying them up. That was it. He walked out. I dragged myself up to a sitting position, itchy from the carpet. I felt sore inside, like he had ripped something, but I didn't want to think about that part of me. A mixture of blood and goo trickled down my inner thigh, and I watched it drip onto the brown carpet and form a tiny puddle.

There I sat, one leg hanging bare with my black sock rolled down around my ankle, and the other leg fully dressed, boot on and everything. I wished so hard that it had never happened.

"Why didn't you tell me, Jane?" Allison asked now, and I knew she was talking about everything.

"I couldn't. I just couldn't."

The room was silent except for a shuffle outside the door. After a few moments Trevor walked in.

"Trev, this must mean congratulations to you, too." Corrine threw her arms around him.

"Yeah, I guess so." He hunched over near the bed.

Although Trevor and I hadn't officially broken up, I knew he wasn't my boyfriend anymore. The only thing we had in common was my secret, and I guess that's why we still talked once in a while. But all we ever said was stuff about Trevor's hockey team or my drama club or dancing. Neither one of us knew what to say about the pregnancy. He hadn't touched me once since he found out it was too late for an abortion. Maybe Trevor was like me, hoping the whole thing would just go away.

"So you went through with it, eh?" Trevor mumbled to me.

Where did that come from?

"You knew that. You were here last night," I said.

"Yeah. Sorry. I didn't mean that."

Then what did you mean?

"Don't tell me she didn't even let you know," Corrine said. "Jane, you must be the queen of secrets."

"She told me. I knew," Trevor snapped.

"Well, she sure as hell didn't tell us," Corrine snarled. "Did you tell *anyone?*"

"No." I felt so bad. I understood why Corrine was angry and why Allison was hurt. "I didn't tell anyone. I'm so sorry. I couldn't."

Allison leaned against my shoulder and said, "It's okay, Jane. We know now and I want to see your baby. Kate told me all about her on the phone."

"Her name is Destiny Mae Williams."

"You're a mom, best friend. How does it feel? Did it hurt? Do you know it is only six weeks until school starts? What are you going to do? Are you coming back to school?" Allison babbled.

"Wait a minute. One question at a time." We giggled self-consciously. "Wanna see her now?" I swung my legs off the bed and pulled on my own housecoat Teh had brought earlier in the day.

Just then a nurse wheeled Destiny's bassinet back into my room. She hung around the door and watched as we passed Destiny back and forth.

"Make sure to support her neck," the nurse said when Trevor handed Destiny to Corrine.

"I'm not a little kid." Corrine was annoyed. "I know how to hold babies."

Trevor peered at his baby's face.

"She's kinda cute ... I guess," he said finally.

"You better say that," I replied. "She looks like you."

"Yeah, I can see that. Sorta has my eyes." He studied the details of Destiny's face. "And maybe my ears too." He got real quiet.

"It's all right, Trev. I'll look after her. Teh and me. My family will be all right. She'll be fine," I said.

"You know I'm moving away soon, don't you?" Trevor said. "To Winnipeg."

"Yeah, I know. I said I'll be fine. We'll be fine."

"My dad said I can't have anything to do with you. Or the baby. He said if you refused to have an abortion then it's your problem."

"Trev, leave it alone. For one thing, she's a baby—not a problem. And we'll be fine without you."

I was glad they had come. I wished I had had the guts to tell them sooner. Especially Allison. I was glad the secret was out. But after they had gone, I was more glad they had left. Most of all, I was glad Trevor was moving away. And his dad.

Trevor's dad had grounded him when he realized Trevor was going out with me, or more to the point, an Indian.

"Stick to one of yours," I overheard his dad tell him one day when I was waiting on the front steps. "And you tell that girl to go home and stick to one of hers."

Trevor had walked out on the porch and said, "Jane, you better go home. I'm not allowed out tonight." From then on Trevor had to sneak around to be with me.

You gutless wonder. Why couldn't you tell me the truth? Bad luck, Mr. Christianson. Your first grandchild, who of course you won't claim, is part Indian.

I knew that the sooner Trevor moved away, the better.

4

"Hey, Baby Jane, it's time to get ready. We're taking you home."
Teh looked happy with her arms full of the deals she found at
her weekend sales. She began emptying the bags and laying
out baby clothes on the bed.

"I washed everything in Ivory and rinsed them in Downy.
Good as new. My great-granddaughter is gonna look like a
princess. It's a good thing Destiny was born on a Friday. That
way I got to the garage sales on the weekend and picked up
everything she's going to need. And then some."

Teh was right about the "and then some." She loved garage
sales.

I remembered the last time we went garage sale-ing was
just two Saturdays before. Uncle Kenny was driving. He sat
in the car while Teh and I walked down one driveway after
another stacked with clothes, books, old record albums, dishes,
small household appliances, and baby furniture. One place
had tables piled high with kids' and baby clothes.

"God, girl, there is nothing I love better than buying baby
clothes. But no one's had a baby for a year or so." Teh had

smiled as she picked over tiny crocheted booties and pink and blue knitted sweaters and bonnets. I gulped and pulled my sweatshirt over my belly. I wanted to get out of there. The baby clothes made me feel creepy, like somehow just from standing next to them Teh would put two and two together and figure it out.

"Garage sales are Indian malls," Teh had said. "There's nothing you can't find and nobody you don't meet up with."

I didn't want to look at baby clothes and I didn't want to meet up with anybody. But sure enough, just as we were squeezing our way through the crowd, lugging a pair of ripped-vinyl-covered bar stools, I turned around and brushed right up against Auntie Pat. She had a startled look on her face when she said, "My girl, you're gonna be as big as me pretty soon if you don't stop putting on the weight."

Teh had flashed her eyes and Auntie didn't say anymore. For a split second I thought for sure she knew. Auntie had five kids of her own and she knew what a pregnant belly felt like. I hurried past the kids' sneakers and baby shoes, tossed my stool in the car, and slunk into the back seat.

"What's wrong with you?" Uncle Kenny asked as he opened one eye.

"Nothing."

"You look like you've seen a ghost," he laughed.

"I'm tired of garage sales. That's all," I said. I held onto my hands to keep them from shaking.

When Teh got into the car she said, "That Pat, she never stops talking about people." That was all she said.

While Teh was still sorting out the baby clothes, Dad came in carrying a car seat.

"Dad," I cried. My heart skipped a beat. I reached my arms out to him. He stepped slowly toward my bed. "Dad, I'm so happy you came. I hardly got to see you the night Destiny was born. I've been waiting for you."

Dad's face was drawn and lined. He seemed older than the last time I saw him. I held my arms suspended toward him, empty, and then slumped them back down on the bed.

"I went and saw the baby in the nursery," he said in barely more than a whisper.

"Her name is Destiny," I said. "Destiny Mae Williams. Isn't she cute?"

"Yes, she's cute. She's got the dark skin. Like you and Mae." A deep V etched across Dad's forehead. "It's sure going to be hard at home. We aren't exactly set up for a baby. It's been fourteen years since we last had a baby in the house."

His eyes were heavy with disappointment. I reached out and picked up his hand. He tried to pull away, but I held on tightly.

"I'm not good with little babies, Jane. It was always your mother."

"I know, Dad."

Dad's eyes filled with tears, and then he said, "I don't think this would have happened if your mom was here."

"I'm sorry for this. I really am. I didn't mean to put you through all this."

I wanted him to say it was okay.

Please, Dad, just say it's okay.

But he didn't. Instead he backed away and I let go of his hand. He stood, his back to me, and looked out the hospital window onto the parking lot.

A nurse came into the room carrying Destiny and laid her on the bed.

"Come on, Jane. Let's dress this little princess in her new clothes." Teh stood proudly over a tiny white sleeper and pair of new socks lying neatly on the bed. She had tucked them together with a hand-knitted pink sweater and bonnet. Dainty white flowers bordered the bonnet, and a white, freshly ironed satin ribbon was tied in a bow. It reminded me of how I laid out my doll clothes when I was a kid.

It was different than other times I had changed Destiny in the hospital. This time was for real. It was a stepping-off point, a springboard, and I was at the end ready to dive in. Part of me wanted to go home, and another part of me wanted to stay in the hospital for a few more days so the nurses could check on Destiny and help me with her.

Destiny didn't want to go home, I could tell. She wiggled and squirmed. I pulled off her hospital nightie and changed her diaper. Her naked body looked like a little frog. Her feet and arms were tucked close to her sides, her toes curled and her fingers clenched in tiny fists.

Loosen up, baby girl. How's Momma going to get you dressed?

My chest tightened. She didn't want me to put on her sleeper.

Is this how babies are supposed to be? Is she in pain?

One voice in my head said, *She's fine. You can do it.* Another voice said, *You're only fourteen. You'll probably screw up. What if you do something wrong and your baby dies?* A third voice, which seemed to be talking to my legs, was confused, telling them to buckle and at the same time to run away. *What are you doing here? There must be some mistake. Get the hell out!*

Destiny's whimpers turned into a cry. Her body stiffened. She poofed her belly out and then sucked it in. I was paralyzed.

Something's wrong with my baby.

Finally my awkward, clumsy hands tugged and pulled her spindly limbs into the sleeper and then the sweater as she screamed at the top of her lungs.

"She doesn't need all those clothes," Dad said as I finally pulled the bonnet onto Destiny's round head. "She's going to swelter."

"He might be right," the nurse agreed. "Just make sure her head is protected from the sun."

Great. I don't even know what my baby needs to wear. She's going to die from heatstroke. I'm not breast-feeding like the nurses want me to so she's probably going to die of food poisoning. I'm all thumbs when I try to bathe her so she's probably going to drown. I'm never going to be able to look after Destiny properly.

My hands trembled as I stuffed a bottle into her mouth and buckled her into her car seat. Teh picked up the bags and the nurse collected the flowers.

"Here, let me take her." Dad picked up the seat and his granddaughter and headed out the door.

I grabbed my knapsack and loosened my belt—the only thing holding up my jeans. The others were already gone as I walked out the door. I turned around and looked at my home for the last four days.

"See ya. I gotta go. On to the next thing." My words echoed across the empty room.

Great-grandmother, grandfather, granddaughter, nurse— shopping bags, blankets, stuffed animals, diapers, flowers, car seat. The hospital hum was now elevator music behind the rustle of bags, the shuffle of shoes, and the grating of pant legs rubbing together. No script, just action. Like in movie promotions where square-jawed actors stride into the picture while bombs explode or guns blast or barely dressed women smoulder in the background. But these actors shuffle, heads down, along the freshly polished floor of a dimly lit hall. A girl trails behind. A girl child. Pudgy and pale. She drags her feet. Her shoulders droop under the weight of her knapsack. Daughter, granddaughter, patient—mother.

As we drove up the cul-de-sac and the car swung into the driveway I looked across the street and saw Mrs. Anderson peering out her window. She jumped back out of sight when my eyes met hers. Mr. Daniels leaned over his fence and talked to Mrs. Underhill, who sat on her lawn chair in her favourite spot near Mr. Daniels' clearing. They craned their necks as the car doors opened.

They were waiting for me. I knew they were. Someone must have told them we were arriving at 12:30 Tuesday afternoon. There was probably a neighbourhood coffee party that morning where they sat around and discussed the Indian girl next door.

Did you hear?

She had a baby. She's only fourteen, you know. I thought she was such a nice girl.

I tried not to think about it. But when I got out of the car I felt the neighbourhood stare penetrating my back like hot needles.

Well, she must be just like the rest of them.

I dropped my head and pulled my hair over my face. I hurried across the driveway, up the front stairs, and into the safety of the front door.

It's really too bad, isn't it. Such a shame. She could have made something out of herself. Now she's got a baby.

The place felt different, but I was home and it was safe now the doors were closed.

It hadn't always felt like home. The cul-de-sac took some getting used to. We lived in Teh's house on the reserve, twenty minutes away, until I was eight. Mom was born in the old house and she was pretty nervous the day we moved to Terrace Avenue.

"I can feel it, Allin," Mom had said. "This neighbourhood doesn't want Indians living here."

"Well, they can just get used to it," Dad told her.

Some of the neighbours didn't mind us moving in because Dad was a white man. But none of us kids looked very white, except Pete. He sort of looked white—he had long, light brown hair. But he wore it in a ponytail and often wore a headband or red bandanna. Otherwise, we all looked like Mom. Especially me.

There were no Indians in the neighbourhood of any sort, not even half Indians, like us. Indians lived on the reserve, a completely different world. And the only thing the white people on Terrace Avenue knew about reserves was that Indians belonged there, not on perfectly good white cul-de-sacs.

Soon after we moved in, Mrs. Anderson warmed up to me. I visited her and helped her with chores around the house. Tuesdays I dragged her garbage out to the street. And then after school I brought her garbage can around to the back of the house. She warmed up to Mom, too, and even brought over a couple of casseroles when Mom got sick, staying a bit to ask Dad how she was doing and stuff like that. Dad was around more then. He came home every night after work and made sure we had dinner before he headed up to the hospital. I helped Dad clean up the house, and the boys listened to him most of the time.

The day before Mom died, Dad and Teh stood beside the hospital bed. Dad said, "Don't worry about us, Mae. I'll look after your children. We'll be all right."

But since that day Dad had sort of walked backward away from the family and into a hidden and gray world of his own. The lines on his face had deepened. He smiled only when he had to. He spoke as few words as possible. I tried to get him to talk—if anyone could squeeze a word out of him it was me. But it took a lot of effort and sometimes I gave up trying.

42

Since then I had understood the order of our family. Dad had been there for Mom, and Mom was there for the family. When Mom passed away, Dad didn't have a hook into us kids anymore. He got so that he was staying in his bedroom most of the time, struggling even to go to work.

Soon Joey and Pete were fulfilling the neighbours' worst expectations. Bernie and Albert, cousins from the reserve, would pull up on weekends in a car full of teenagers. Toronto Maple Leafs games Saturday nights on TV often turned pretty rowdy. By the 7 p.m. game finish, most of them were usually so drunk or stoned they couldn't drive home. So they'd stay and party, spilling out into the backyard, driveway, and down the cul-de-sac until long after midnight. Often the police came and broke it up, and it was usually Mr. Underhill who called them. It got so he'd be calling them as soon as Bernie's old '72 Dodge Monaco pulled in the driveway, or as soon as he heard Albert's lowered Lincoln turn the corner.

One day I ran into him on my way home from school.

"Afternoon," he said.

"Good afternoon," I said.

"I've been watching you, girl, and I think you're better than your brothers. You make sure you keep going to school. The only way for someone like you to get ahead is to get a good education." There was a critical drip in his voice that made what was meant to be a compliment into an insult.

I finally called Teh and asked her to come over. I had just turned twelve and I knew I couldn't look after the family on my own. "We need your help, Teh. Remember you promised you would look after us if we missed Mom too much."

That same afternoon Teh dragged her suitcases up the front stairs and into the spare bedroom, where she'd stayed ever since. And Dad just stayed around the edges of the family.

"It takes a long time," Teh told me, "to get over losing someone you love. Especially if you love them as much as Allin loved Mae."

Coming home from the hospital, it seemed like nothing had changed. The boys hadn't cleaned up the house. Music blared from the basement. The neighbours still peered down their noses at us. But one really important thing would never be the same again. I was no longer the good Williams. I was now the girl who had a baby. I knew it. I could tell from the stretch of their necks, the fingers pulling back the curtains, and the we-knew-it-all-along air that plugged up the house even though our door was shut.

I stumbled up the stairs. Shoes were scattered inside the door, papers and magazines stacked in piles on either side of the staircase, and sweatshirts hung on the banister. But someone had piled the dishes in the sink and put the food away. The peanut butter jar wasn't on the counter, there was no bread or cheese or crackers strewn across the table, and there were no beer cans packed in the corner.

"Welcome home!" Pete, Joey, and Kate jumped into the hallway. They had been hiding in the bathroom. Pete clutched a bunch of balloons with "Congratulations!" written across them, Joey had a bouquet of tulips, and Kate held a huge stuffed teddy bear.

"Welcome home, Baby Jane and Baby Destiny." Pete swung his arms around me wildly.

"Thank you, guys. I'm glad to be home."

"Yeah, man, welcome back to the place." Joey kissed my cheeks. "We forgive you for not warning us that we were going to be uncles, and we're happy you're home. Both of you."

Kate stuffed the teddy bear next to Destiny and then sat beside us on the sofa.

"Jane, you're awesome, girl. I can't believe you did this all on your own. Are you okay?" Kate stroked Destiny's tiny smooth head. "She's so beautiful."

"Thanks." Up until then, Kate was Joey's girlfriend. She never had time for me. In fact, she stayed out of my way as much as possible and spent most of her time in the family room or the boys' room. Now she looked right at me.

"It's going to be okay, Jane. I know it will be. Teh will help. I'll help. I know Joey and Pete will be there for you."

"Thanks, Kate."

"Can I pick her up?" Kate asked.

"Sure."

Kate fumbled with the car seat buckle, trying cautiously to free Destiny from the straps.

"Here, like this," I said as I lifted Destiny into her arms.

"Wow. You're already a mom," she said.

5

When I was a kid I used to sit on the stairs of the old house and listen to Teh talk to visitors. They came in a steady stream, each with a glitch in their life they wanted her to fix. She'd listen and nod. She would commiserate with some, and at other times she would set the visitor straight on one detail or another. She'd change her words a bit for different people, sometimes talking about paddling your own canoe, other times about carving your own pole. But she always spoke with the same rhythm.

I wrote a poem in grade eight using her words:

make your own trail
use the stuff you got
the ground under your feet
the air that flies your kite
the people around you
it's all there
remember
you set your sails, turn your wheel, adjust your rudder, tune
*   your strings*
nobody else can do it

wisdom will help you
listen to the wind
slow down at corners
stay awake on long straight stretches
watch out for potholes
and
step softly like a dancer
with eagle feathers and tin bells and glass beads

Now I finally knew what those words meant. A few of my decisions had set me up for the rest of my life. First, I decided to have sex with Trevor. It didn't feel like a decision at the time. It felt more like I was on the back of a train and ended up where the front car was headed. It was more that I *didn't* make a decision *not* to have sex with him. And two negatives don't make a positive. Not when it comes to having sex. So my first non-decision decision forced me to make the next decision, not to have an abortion.

Trevor had got all the information—the doctor that I needed to see, how much it would cost, and how long it would take. He thought having an abortion was my only choice. If I didn't, he said, I would ruin my life, and his, which was the part I think he was worried about. I said no abortion. The decision was easy. My brain and my heart and my instinct came together at the same time and just said no abortion. I made another decision at the same time—no one was going to take my baby away from me. And a third, crazy one—that I was going to keep the whole thing a secret.

The decisions were easy. But I didn't think about the consequences, not really. I never thought about what my choices were going to mean. Not until after Destiny was born.

47

Then my life became a whole bunch of questions, choices, consequences.

Like the decision whether or not I would breast-feed. I couldn't imagine pulling my breasts out and having a baby suck on them, not even Destiny, so I decided to bottle-feed her. That meant I had to worry about whether she was going to be all right with store-bought milk or whether she'd have allergies and get sick. The nurse helped me decide what formula to feed her, and Teh helped me decide to use disposable diapers instead of washable ones. But I had to decide where Destiny would sleep and what to do with her when she was awake for hours at a time.

Then I had to make little decisions every minute. Decisions like whether to pick her up or leave her for a few minutes when she cried. I had to decide whether she was crying because she was wet or hungry or because she had gas or because she was sick or because she was tired or . . . ? It never let up.

The first day of school was six weeks after Destiny was born and I had to decide whether I should go back to school or stay home and look after Destiny. There were so many things to think about. What's best for Destiny? What's best for me? What will happen if I go back? What will happen if I don't? I wanted Teh to tell me what was best, but she said I had to decide. I didn't want to stay home all day, and it seemed that the right thing to do was go back to school. I figured I should start in September, as usual, and try to keep up with the other kids my age.

My high school had a daycare, a cool little building at the end of the student parking lot. As soon as I got pregnant I had started noticing the girls coming and going, pushing strollers and packing babies and diaper bags. They usually looked tired and grumpy. I dreaded being one of them so, like everything else, I ignored the daycare and looked the other way whenever I was near. Now it felt pretty weird to think of being one of the young mothers. At first the supervisor said Destiny was too young to attend. Then she called us back and said they had decided Destiny could be admitted and that she would see us on September 6.

When the summer holidays were over I didn't feel rested or that I'd had a holiday. I hadn't had a good night's sleep since Destiny was born. I still couldn't button my jeans, and my breasts, although they'd stopped leaking, hung like melons, hard, lumpy, and sore. On the first day of school I caught a glimpse of myself as I passed the full-length mirror attached to the wall of my bedroom.

God. I was wearing the same sweatshirt that I wore every day until Destiny was born. The letters on the front were peeled and faded. *Slow Pitch Champions, 2001.* I stepped closer to the mirror. I had always wanted to look older, mature, sophisticated. Well, that morning I certainly did look older, in the way people look when they have lived so long they are tired of it. The look that pulls at the corner of your eyes and sucks at the colour of your skin.

I stayed there, mesmerized, seeing at the same time the face of a twelve year old. A roll of baby fat hung below my chin, my cheeks were round and plump, and I still had that it-wasn't-me look in my eyes, the look Pete and Joey said got them in trouble even if it *was* me that started something. I grabbed my cheeks with my palms, squinted, and pressed my fingers into my eyes. When I pulled my hands away from my face I stared blankly at myself.

The girl mother is going to school with her baby.

I walked out of my room and met Kate in the hall.

"Don't worry about it, Jane," Kate said. I jostled the diaper bag I had packed the night before and tried to pick up my knapsack. "The school's daycare is just for girls like you."

"What do you mean, 'for girls like me'?" I asked. I felt like I had been broadsided by a pickup truck. Even Kate thought of me as a "girl like that."

One of those girls in the daycare.

"I'm sorry, I didn't mean anything. It's just that you're lucky. O'Neil High has a daycare and that's good for you and Destiny," Kate said as she buckled Destiny into the car seat.

"I don't feel lucky," I said. My stomach felt lumpy and tense. Usually on the first day of school I couldn't wait to see everyone. But that morning I felt like crawling back into bed. "I don't know if I have any friends. Allison's been over a few times, but Corrine hasn't. I've had a few phone calls, but no one knows what to say."

"I'm back at school this year," Kate said. "I'll be there."

"Thanks. I'm going to need you. Even the teachers will look at me funny. I've hardly been out of the house since Destiny was born. Now I have to face everyone at once."

"Okay, Jane. Got your bag packed? Ready to go?" Joey jingled the car keys. "I'm taking my girls to school."

"You should be coming with us, Joey. Why aren't you going back this year?" I asked.

"Maybe later. I'm going to find a job." Joey lifted Destiny's car seat and went out.

When I walked out the front door I didn't glance to see if Mrs. Anderson was pulling her curtain or if Mr. Underhill was craning his neck. All I thought about was the stone that sat in the pit of my stomach and my chest tightening around my breath. In the car I yawned to get oxygen into my lungs, but the air got stuck. I gulped big mouthfuls of air and then tried to force it down my throat.

"You all right, little sister?" Joey asked.

"No, not really," I said. My eyes stung. "I'm scared. I want to turn around and go back home. Can I come back with you and watch TV?"

Joey twisted his neck and glared at me over the front seat. "No way, man. You aren't going to do that. You aren't quitting school, Jane. Never, no way. You're not like me."

You're not like me.

I used to be sure that I wasn't like Joey or Pete. Everyone told me that. They were rowdies. I was straight. I was smart. I was a good student. I never missed one day of middle school, from grade six to grade eight. I got the perfect attendance award when I graduated to high school. I was a good girl. I never drank, not even when Allison and Corrine tried it. I never smoked dope. I never stayed out late or talked back to Dad or Teh. I didn't even swear. But now what difference did that make? I knew that everyone who looked at me would be thinking of only one thing, and I knew what it was.

I sank deep into the back seat as Joey pulled the car up in front of the daycare. Kids dressed in the latest fall clothes sauntered around the parking lot. At first no one paid attention to the green 1975 Mustang, but the longer I sat, the more kids slowed down and peered in the window.

"Come on, Jane," Kate said. "You have to do it. I'll come with you."

She opened the door, jumped out, and pulled the seat forward. She hauled the diaper bag out of the back seat and waited.

"Come on. It's going to be okay," she reassured me.

I stumbled out of the car as Joey picked up Destiny. By this time students, gathered in small groups, were twisting their necks and looking at us. I hunched over, dropped my head, and walked in a straight line to the daycare. The door opened just as I reached the porch.

"Welcome, Jane. And Destiny. Come on in." Karen, the daycare supervisor, greeted us with a friendly smile. She took Destiny from Joey. Kate and I followed her into the office.

"We have eight babies this year and Destiny is the youngest. You're such a tiny baby," she sang in baby talk and poked Destiny's nose. "You'll have to make extra sure you come in during break and lunch every day," she said, looking back at me. "You'll get used to it. Now, is there a daddy who will also be visiting Destiny?"

"No."

"If anyone else is going to come and visit we'll need their name and your signature for approval."

"Just me," Kate volunteered. "I'll help."

After I signed Kate's name to the list, Karen told me the rules. I had heard them all when Teh and I registered Destiny, but it was good to hear them again. There were so many things to remember. Bottles, baby food, diapers, sign in, sign out, emergencies, the phone, the sleeping room, the playroom, birth control education, parenting classes, psychologists, university student observers, health lectures.

"This is going to be your second home, Jane. I want you to feel comfortable here." Karen explained that she had had a baby herself when she was seventeen. That sounded pretty old to me, but Karen said she knew just how I felt.

"Any questions?"

"No, I'll figure it out."

"I guess you girls better run. You must have a lot to do with it being the first day of school."

I kissed Destiny and stroked her downy hair. "Wish me luck, baby girl. I'm going to need it."

"You'll be fine." Kate grabbed my hand. "Come on, let's get going."

"She's got everything she needs," I said to Karen. I didn't want to leave. It felt safe in the daycare. I wasn't ready to face the parking lot between me and the school. "I've never left her before with anybody."

"She's fine with me," Karen assured me. "That's what I'm here for."

"I'll be back around ten."

"Sounds like you got it together, girl," Karen said.

"I don't look it," I said as I scanned myself in the mirror by the door. I rewrapped my ponytail, yanked on my jeans to loosen their grip on my thighs, and adjusted my breasts in my bra.

Kate dragged me out the door. I dug my heels in.

I don't want to go. This wasn't a good idea. I should be at home with Destiny.

The parking lot was almost empty. Most kids had congregated around the front door of the school. I looked through the crowd to try to find Allison and Corrine, but I couldn't see anyone I wanted to talk to. The calm I felt in my stomach while I was in the daycare evaporated when I saw the crowd.

You are the same girl that came to school last year. They are the same kids.

But nothing was the same and I knew it. The parking lot stood between who I used to be at O'Neil High and who I had become.

The girl with a baby.

I used to be popular. I hung around with the in crowd—dancers and singers, the drama club, basketball and soccer jocks. Trevor and his friends even said I was hot. Now I felt sick to my stomach, terrified. I hunched forward and wrapped my arms around myself.

"I can't do it, Kate," I said. "I just can't do it."

"Come on, Jane, you have to. In a day or two it'll be all over. It'll be fine." Kate put her hand on my shoulder. "Come on, girl. You can do it."

If my body could have coiled up like a snail's I would have backed into my shell and disappeared. Kate tugged on my arm. I stumbled forward. It felt like a headwind was blowing in my face and like my pants were caught on the fence, pulling me back. When I got near the jumble of noise and commotion I couldn't move.

"Hold on a minute, Kate," I said. "I'll get it together."

I felt numb.

I scanned my scrambled brain looking for courage, for guts, for power. I was looking for a kick in the butt or for someone to grab hold of me and drag me up to the front door and toss me inside. I needed something to stop me from sitting down on the warm morning pavement, pulling my sweatshirt over my face, and bawling.

"Come on, Jane." Kate tugged gently.

"One minute, Kate, please."

I thought of Teh. She's the kind of woman who knows what she knows, not from reading magazines or from watching talk shows, but from, as she says, plain living life and then thinking about it.

Last night while I packed the diaper bag, she had plopped herself on my bed, folded her hands, and said, "Jane." I knew she had something to say. And I knew it wasn't about doing the dishes or laundry. She was going to tell me a story about life.

"Jane," she said again. "You know, girl, I was thinking. Life has a way of getting to people in ways they don't understand, and at times they aren't ready. I've seen people drop their head like this"—she flopped her head down on her chest—"they're feeling so bad about something. They're so depressed that they forget to pick it up. Not later that day or the next day."

Teh stopped talking for a bit, as if she was deciding how to finish the story. Then she continued. "You know, girl, I've seen people keep their head down all the way to their graves. I'm surprised they don't trip over their casket. Lots of us Indians, granddaughter, have been just like that. Heads down, eyes down, feeling down. But we're figuring it's time to pick up our chins, look up, straight ahead, all around. The Williams aren't the kind of people to be flopping our heads around." She bent her neck down again and wagged her head like it was on a swivel.

"We aren't the kind of people that keep our necks bent, looking down at the ground. Not us."

Not us.

A young girl staggers across the student parking lot. Her shoulders stoop, her belly sags, her boobs droop, and so do her eyes and the corners of her lips. She curls forward into a ball. Smaller and smaller as she nears the crowd. Until she is a tiny speck.

I exhaled until there wasn't a flicker of air in my lungs. Then I opened my mouth and drew air into my belly. As the air filled my chest, my shoulders rolled back and my chin lifted a little. I looked up. A few dry maple leaves loosened and crackled as they collided with a branch while they drifted to the pavement.

Dig deep, Jane. You come from a line of strong women.

My feet were like lead weights when I tried to walk—I bent my knees. My stomach muscles were mush—I flexed, slightly. I raised my chin bit by bit and stretched my neck from side to side—I heard a gentle pulling. I breathed dry grass and overripe blackberries deep into my lungs. Suddenly a wave of something very clear washed over me.

I am going to create my trail. I am going to walk right into the crowd.

I rolled my shoulders back.

It's me who sets my sails and turns my wheel. No one is there for me except me. No one is there for my baby except me.

I tightened my jaw and tilted my chin up.

If I'm not confident, they will treat me like trash.

I breathed the cool air. It tingled through my veins.

I'm going to step like a dancer, with eagle feathers and tin bells and glass beads.

I lifted my feet, step by step, toward the school, through the crowd, in the front door, and down the hall. Stares burned into my skin. Through the cacophony of words and conversation, certain voices rang clear.

"Look, that's the girl with a baby."

"Yeah, that's her. And no one even knew she was pregnant."

"She doesn't look any different."

"I think she does. She's kind of fatter, don't you think?"

Kate and I stopped at the lunchroom.

"That's harsh," Kate exclaimed. "Did you hear what they were saying?"

"Yeah, but I'm okay now, Kate. Thanks for being here for me."

After Kate found her friends, we separated and I continued down the hall. I found Allison and Corrine standing with a crowd of kids in the corner next to the science labs—our favourite spot.

"Hi, guys."

"Hey, you," Allison called out. "You look great, Jane. Do you like my new jeans? I lost eight pounds this summer. Pretty sexy, eh?"

"Yeah, you look good," I said. I hadn't thought about sexy jeans, not for a long time.

Corrine turned her shoulder away from me and began to talk to Vanessa.

What's Vanessa doing hanging around with Allison and Corrine?

Vanessa seemed out of place at O'Neil High. I had always imagined she should go to Queen Elizabeth, the private school, or North Valley Collegiate, where the high-class people sent their kids. She stood a head taller than me and a good bit taller than everyone else too. Her silky blond hair hung in twists down her back. Her skin was smooth and velvety and almost as dark as mine, but not from Indian blood. Her skin was the result of tanning, careful tanning to make sure she didn't get any lines, anywhere. I didn't remember Vanessa ever having braces, but she had the large straight white teeth of the smiling mouths in Hollywood magazines. And as if she didn't tower over everyone enough already, she always wore heels at least four or five inches high. She could walk in them, and run, like Julia Roberts—even up and down stairs.

I didn't know why she was so interested in me that morning. She looked tight and agitated, watching me out of the corner of her eye as she talked.

"So," she finally spoke to me, "I guess you won't be in musical theatre this year, eh, Jane? Too bad, we're doing *Grease*. And I guess you won't have time for drama club— now you've had a *baby*."

Then I knew. Although Vanessa ruled when it came to the halls of O'Neil High and I was a nobody compared to her,

I seemed to threaten her when it came to musical theatre. She had never forgotten the grade five musical production when I played the Prince and she played Snow White. With my hair tucked under a cap, singing her a love song, I ended up getting more attention than her. Vanessa wasn't the kind of girl to get over things like that.

"Yeah, I had a baby."

Saved by the bell.

6

It was quiet in the house and chilly for the first week of October. I heard the furnace clunk and grind for the first time that fall. The nightlight at the end of the bed cast a yellow glow through the bedroom. I swayed my hips from side to side, my special put-Destiny-to-sleep rhythm. She whined a low sleepy cry and wiggled and twisted her tummy, like her head wanted to be asleep but the rest of her didn't. I wrapped my arms snugly around her and sang the lullaby over and over. Soon I heard Mom's voice slivering through the night air.

Go to sleep, my dear baby.

Close your eyes now, dream away.

Dream of butterflies, bees, and hummingbirds.

I listened and I sang.

Dream of ice cream and Smarties.

I knew it was Mom. I closed my eyes and remembered Mom and me sitting at the kitchen table in front of huge bowls of Neapolitan ice cream covered in Smarties—they were her favourites.

"Come on, little girl, go to sleep," I pleaded with Destiny. "Mommy's still got to read ten pages for history and make a title page for my English report. "

Destiny gnawed angrily on her fist. She jerked her head from side to side and scrunched her knees up tight to her tummy. Her body was tense with pain and her cries became increasingly irritated.

"Come on, baby girl. What's wrong with you? What can I do?"

The red numbers on the clock radio turned over to 11:00 and then 11:10 and 11:20.

"Baby, it's late. Please don't wake up Teh. And now I'm too tired to do my homework."

Destiny squeezed her eyes tight shut and shrieked. I was getting nervous and impatient, but mostly I was tired and drained. I had nothing left.

"Please, baby girl, I don't know what you want."

Destiny had cried before. Sometimes she cried for so long that I got really mad at her. But tonight was different. I felt a racing inside my chest, my blood surged until I could hear my pulse, and my bones vibrated.

"Stop it, Destiny! I am doing everything I can. Just stop it!"

She curled in a cramped ball and wailed.

Lullaby and good night . . .

I sang it again. My voice was ratty, loud, and agitated. I tried to comfort Destiny with a gentle sway of my hips, but instead they snapped irritably back and forth. Panic mounded inside like a storm gathering.

"Stop! Please stop. Your mommy doesn't know what to do. I can't do this much longer. I'm going to collapse."

My hands, arms, and legs started to shake. There was a buzz behind my ears and a boil in my blood. My incredible love for my baby got mixed up with exhaustion, frustration, and fear. Everything whirled around me—out of control.

"Stop it, Destiny," I shouted. "You stop it. Right now." My arms clenched tightly around her. I squeezed her. "Stop crying, you're driving me crazy!" I kept squeezing her until her scream thinned to a squeak.

It's too much for me, baby. I can't do this. I'm so sorry, baby girl.

She gasped for breath. My brain scrambled. I locked my arms around her little body.

I'm sorry. I'm sorry.

Finally I fell onto my bed and dropped Destiny beside me. She gulped air and was silent. Finally she gulped again and let out a scream. I curled my body around her and cried. I cried so hard and loud I couldn't hear Destiny anymore, only the pain sounds from my own hysteria.

"Jane! Jane!" Teh shook my shoulder. "Girl, what's wrong with you?" She rolled me over and rubbed her hands on my cheeks. "I'm here, Jane. Come on, calm down."

Teh picked up Destiny.

"Oh, I can feel cramps in your little tummy, baby girl," Teh said as she laid Destiny over her shoulder. "And your mommy is too tired to know what to do with you."

"I can't do it, Teh," I sobbed. "I'm too scared."

"She's got gas, honey. Every baby gets gas. And every mother gets scared."

Teh sat down and stroked my forehead with one hand as she rubbed Destiny's back with the other. "I got something for her tummy. Come on, I'll find it."

I followed Teh and Destiny into the bathroom.

"Gripe water. It's the answer. Your mother used it on you. It'll work for Destiny. Go get me a little spoon."

Teh poured the medicine into Destiny's mouth while she spewed it back out until Teh decided Destiny had had enough.

Gradually Destiny's body relaxed. She stretched her arms and legs out and lay peacefully in Teh's arms.

"You all right now, Jane?"

"Yeah. I'll be fine."

"Let my great-grandbaby sleep with me tonight. You go to bed and have a good night's rest."

"No, it's okay, Teh." I made a feeble attempt to resist. "She can sleep with me."

"I said you go to bed, Granddaughter. Destiny is sleeping with me."

I was still shaking when I hugged Teh and said, "Thanks. Destiny says thanks too."

It had got away on me. It had been too much. Way too much. I sat on the edge of my bed, terrified. I folded my arms around myself to stop the shakes. All I could hear was my teeth chattering.

Don't ever get to that out-of-control place again. I'm so sorry, baby. I will never hurt you. Never.

I rolled up Destiny's little bed, the blankets, towels, and pillows that lay next to me. I shook my bedspread and fluffed my pillows and lay spread-eagled across the bed. I heard my heart beating as I sank deep into the mattress. I was exhausted but not sleepy. I wanted to pray, but I didn't know a god to pray to so I thought hard about my grandmothers, the old women through the ages of my family, the ones Teh talked about in her stories—until I fell asleep.

A young woman sits on a cedar stump beside a tiny ramshackle hut. A red kerchief binds her hair. Her calico skirt hangs limp and dusty over her heavy black boots tied up to her shins. Her fingers toss tufts of white fleece and deftly filter out dirt, twigs, and brambles. A tiny baby, bound tightly on a buckskin board, leans against the trunk of a maple tree near the woman and sleeps soundly.

Another baby, one year old, maybe two, draws images in the dust with a whittled alder branch. The woman's face is smooth like velvet. Her eyes are serene when she looks up. Two young girls, five or six years old, twins, identical, say "Mommy."

I fiddled with my lock in the hall.

"I can help," Allison said. "They suck. I can get those things open better without the combination."

I finally yanked it open.

"Thanks anyway."

"You going to the drama club meeting after school?" Allison asked.

"Yeah, I hope so."

"You should've been at the basketball game last night. We beat Lakewood. Jason was awesome. And he talked to me after the game." Allison danced around, still high on the attention.

"Oh yeah, the basketball game. As if I could go out. I haven't left Destiny yet with anybody—just the daycare," I replied.

"Yeah, I guess so. Sorry I didn't think of that," Allison went on. "There was a party at Lisa's place on Friday. I wish you could have come out with us. You should have seen Corrine. She was in the weirdest mood and she had way too much to drink. She wouldn't leave the guys alone. She flirted with everyone's boyfriend. I had to get her out of there before she got the crap kicked out of her."

Parties seemed like a long time ago—like another world. Another life. I felt stupid. Allison was my best friend, but I couldn't think of what to say. I couldn't say, "I wish I was there," because I really didn't. I couldn't say, "I'm glad Corrine didn't get the crap kicked out of her," because I didn't really care that much about it. There was a blank spot. But I wanted more than anything to talk to Allison. I wanted to find something to say that we could talk about all afternoon and into the evening like we used to.

I could tell Allison wished we could talk forever as well, but all she said was, "I miss you, Jane."

"Why don't you come over sometime?" I said. "We can paint our toenails. And wax our legs. You can get to know Destiny. She's a real sweetie, you know."

"Yeah, I know she is." Allison looked away. "It's my fault. I should come over and spend time with you guys."

"No, it's not your fault at all."

"Corrine never wants to go over to your place. She says you've changed. And for some reason I just never get around to it."

"It's okay, Allison. I guess I have changed. It's not like I have a lot of choice."

Allison hugged me. It kind of felt like before. Like we were still best friends. "I think you're doing a good job," she said. "You are so strong. Destiny's lucky to have such a good mom."

Destiny is lucky to have such a good mom.

Teh had told me I was doing a good job. And Dad had said just a few days before that I was going to be a good mom. Like it was going to happen sometime in the future . . . but I took it as a compliment, especially coming from Dad. I had never thought that Destiny was lucky to have me for a mom. I only thought of how unlucky Destiny was having a teenage, single mom. People on TV shows talked about how children with teenage moms were more likely to be poor, uneducated, to have bad teeth and medical problems, to become criminals, to get low grades in school, have a bad diet and low self-esteem. You name it. They go on and on. I had never heard one positive thing about teenage motherhood. And I didn't have a lot of positive stuff to say about it either.

But every day when I picked Destiny up at the daycare, she smiled at me. It wasn't one of those funny faces—she looked in my eyes like no one had ever looked at me before. Not even Mom. And when she smiled—wow—I knew for sure that I loved her with all my heart. I knew whether we ended up rich or poor, Destiny was going to be loved like no other kid in the world. I knew no matter how hard it was, I was meant to be her mom.

Maybe Destiny is lucky to have me for a mom.

I slung my knapsack and the diaper bag over my shoulder and pushed Destiny, strapped in her stroller, into the drama room. A few dozen kids hung around in small groups, talking and laughing. Allison and Corrine stood on the stage behind Vanessa, who was talking to Mr. Knight, the drama teacher. I sat down and pushed the stroller in front of my seat. I packed the bags neatly beside us so we didn't take up too much space.

"Quiet, everyone," Mr. Knight called the meeting to order. "It's good to see so much interest. Glad to see so many of you here for the first meeting about our musical production. I have great news. After a lot of work and spending a lot of money we were able to get the rights to play *Grease* this year. Thanks to a whole bunch of people."

By then most of the kids had sat down. The room had settled into an expectant quiet.

"Most of you know that last June we voted for a new drama club president. Now I'm pleased to announce the winner—Vanessa Richardson." He turned to her and said, "Do you want to say a few words?"

"Thanks, Mr. Knight." Vanessa walked to the centre of the stage. "Let's hear a round of applause for Mr. Knight, who worked so hard to get us *Grease*. Yeah." There was a loud roar. Vanessa was good with a crowd. She knew how to turn heads and get everyone to pay attention. "We have some great ideas for the drama club. We're going to be fundraising all year so we can buy new props and awesome costumes. Meetings are every Wednesday afternoon and we want everyone working this year. No slackers. I'm going to make sure of that. So next Wednesday I'll see you right here at three o'clock sharp."

Instead of leaving the stage, Vanessa sat down and dangled her legs while Mr. Knight continued.

"We're starting early this year, folks, because we intend this to be the best program the O'Neil High Junior Musical Theatre Group has ever produced. Auditions will be held February 1 and 2. From now until then in practices we'll concentrate on building skills—acting, singing, and dancing. The technical crew will be working on improving our lighting, audio, and prop capacity, and we'll be working hard at fundraising. Vanessa has a lot of good ideas about raising money—bottle drives, car washes, sponsorships. I want you all to put in a full effort and make this production your production. Let's do it!"

Mr. Knight shouted the last part. Startled, Destiny's eyes sprang open and she let out a squeal. I pushed the stroller back and forth with my foot, hoping she would go back to sleep. Instead she grumbled louder and louder until she broke into a loud cry. I fumbled around in the diaper bag.

Oh, please, let there be a full bottle in here. I can't miss this meeting.

I pulled out spare sweaters, sleepers, diapers, diaper wipes, baby towels, everything I didn't need. I dug around impatiently until I found three empty bottles and one bottle half full of formula. I stuffed the bottle in Destiny's mouth and she guzzled so loudly that kids turned around and watched. Vanessa glared at me and then smirked, as if she enjoyed my frustration.

Mr. Knight finished talking to the technical people, then dismissed everyone but the actors. By this time Destiny had finished her bottle and started to complain again. She wasn't crying—yet—but her voice was loud and demanding and I could tell she was hungry. I picked her up and jostled her on my hip.

How can I keep you quiet, baby? Please give Mommy a bit more time.

Vanessa stood up and walked back to centre stage. Staring at me, she said, "Can we have quiet in here? We're supposed to be a professional acting troupe. Mr. Knight isn't finished."

Destiny got louder and louder, and there was nothing I could do to keep her quiet so I packed her in the stroller. As I picked up my knapsack and diaper bag and headed toward the door, I felt a hand on my back.

I swung around and saw a girl, not much taller than me. She had blond hair, cropped ear-length and clumpy. Other than the ring in her nose and the tattoo of lips on her neck, she looked sporty. Her legs were thick, like a soccer or hockey player's. I imagined her wearing a karate *gi* with a black belt.

"Hey, I'm part of the lighting crew and we're out of here," she said. "If you need to stay, I'd be glad to look after your baby for awhile."

I looked at her in disbelief.

"It's okay. I used to babysit all the time. I love babies." She poked Destiny on her nose. "You're a hungry baby," she cooed.

"No, but thanks. It's a great offer. But I don't know you,"

I stammered. I couldn't leave Destiny with someone I had never met, but I didn't want to sound ungrateful and I needed to attend the rest of the meeting.

"You live on Terrace Avenue?" she asked.

"Yeah."

"Then I'm your neighbour you haven't met yet. I moved in just up the street from you. My mom said there was a girl with a baby on our street somewhere. That must be you. Here, let me take the stroller out in the hall. I'll wait for you and we can walk home together."

She picked up the diaper bag and started to push the stroller and Destiny toward the door.

I watched them walk away.

Sometimes I can trust people right off. I don't need to ask questions. This girl was like that, but that didn't mean I felt completely okay about her taking my baby. "The meeting will only be a few more minutes, I think," I called after her.

As the door closed behind them I stood empty-handed, without Destiny.

What if she packs Destiny into a car and takes off? What if someone else is waiting outside ready to whisk her away?

I opened the drama room door a crack and watched the girl walking down the hall.

"Oh, little girl, we're just waiting for your mommy, don't be a grumpy," I overheard her say as Destiny gurgled and snorted.

I shut the door, took a chair, and settled back to listen.

"I want you all to know what's expected of you," Mr. Knight said. "We want this production to be the best ever. We want you guys to work as hard as you can and to try out for the best role you can. You have lots of time to learn, and we're going to be as fair as possible.

"Any questions?" He paused and then continued, "We'll

try to make sure everyone has a fair chance to get the parts. The judges will have three criteria. Listen very closely. Number one: We will be looking for technical ability. This means you are a good singer, a good dancer, a good actor. That means everyone practises. Nobody is so good they don't need to improve. Number two: We want actors with enthusiasm. That means you put your heart and soul into the performance. It means you want to be here. It means you're not just acting the part, you're living it. Number three: We'll be looking for actors with attitude. Good attitude. That means you're cooperative, easy to work with, and generous with the other actors. That means no prima donnas.

"Any questions?" Mr. Knight never waited long for questions. "Good. We will be assessing you throughout the practice season. I want to see you all here, every time. If schoolwork gets in the way, let me know."

I started to worry about Destiny again and edged my way to the door.

I don't even know the girl's name. I have never seen her before.

"Okay, gang, see you all here at three next Wednesday."

I turned and rushed out the door. The girl was pushing the stroller back toward the drama room while Destiny sat fast asleep.

"She forgot she was hungry when I took her for a walk around the school," the girl said. "We went exploring. I don't know my way around here either."

"Thank you very much. I really didn't want to miss that meeting," I said.

"No problem. Glad to help. My name is Dawna. Dawna Morgan."

"Hi, I'm Jane. Jane Williams. And this is Destiny Mae Williams."

"That's a beautiful name for a beautiful baby girl. She looks like you." Dawna passed over the stroller. "Are you walking home?"

"Yes," I replied. "I usually get a ride home from my brother Joey when he comes to pick up his girlfriend. But he won't wait for me if I stay late after school."

"Come on then, neighbour." Dawna picked up the diaper bag and walked toward the door.

7

"Come on, Destiny, bend your arm," I begged. Destiny always seemed to decide to be stubborn when I was in a hurry. Just like when I was a kid playing with my Barbie dolls. Bone-stiff arms and legs, and me just wishing they would bend.

The doorbell rang. I heard the door open. It was Dawna. She'd been hitching a ride with us for a week now.

"Hey! Coming, ready or not. Let's go." She grabbed the diaper bag, stuffed it full of bottles and diapers, and said, "Joey's waiting in the car. He says we have one second to get out to the car or he's leaving without us."

It had taken Dawna no time at all to get to know everyone. She was the kind of girl who seemed to have both feet firmly placed wherever she was standing. She had a confidence that made you feel like you had known her forever.

Joey gunned the engine and the Mustang backfired twice before we pulled up the road.

"Kate?" I asked hesitantly. "I have a really big favour to ask you."

"Ask away," she replied.

"Drama club is starting regular meetings this week. We'll

be practising for the *Grease* production, and I really want to get a good part," I said.

"And you want me to babysit," Kate said. "When are the practices?"

"After school on Wednesdays. Until about five o'clock," I said. It was the first time I had ever asked anyone to babysit before. Dad and Teh filled in at home sometimes when I needed a rest or I had homework to do, but I had never needed a babysitter.

"You want Kate to babysit every Wednesday?" Joey asked.

"Yeah, if I'm going to get a good part I need to be there with no interruptions," I said. "Every week."

Since Joey and Kate got together, Joey took care of things. He decided where they went and when they would get there. Kate usually stood a few steps behind him and nodded or frowned.

"Maybe Kate's busy on Wednesdays," Joey said.

"I can speak for myself here, don't you think?" Kate said in a way that surprised everyone.

She hesitated, staring wordlessly at her hands with their gnawed and bitten fingernails.

"You know what?" she finally said to Joey. "I don't like you answering for me."

I didn't know what that meant in terms of the babysitting, but it was pretty weird to see Kate speaking up for herself.

"I'm my own person and I'll decide what I want to do for myself," she carried on.

We were in the school parking lot by then, but Joey just sat there silently.

"I was just thinking you might not want to babysit," he said at last, wanting to back away from a confrontation.

"Yeah, well, why were you thinking that?"

"Kate, don't get all messed up about it. It's not some big deal."

"Yeah, well, maybe it is for me."

I waited through another long pause, still wondering about the babysitting.

"Thanks, Jane," Kate finally said. "I'd love to look after Destiny. I wondered when you would ask me. I thought you didn't trust me or something."

"No, no, it's not that. I just feel so bad asking people. I know you guys got things to do and stuff."

"Nothing more important than looking after Destiny," Kate said.

When Joey opened the Mustang door, Kate reached into the back seat and unbuckled Destiny from her car seat.

"Come on, baby girl. Come with Auntie Kate."

You could tell from the way Joey tightened his lips and closed one eye that he wasn't too sure what to think about Kate's new self-assertion or the idea of "Auntie Kate."

When I arrived at the daycare on Wednesday afternoon, Kate and Joey were already waiting outside with Destiny packed in the back of the car, ready to go.

"I'll be home around five. Is that okay?"

"Great, she'll be fine. Don't worry."

When I watched the car pull away I suddenly felt empty. I wanted to pick something up and hold it in my hand or eat something. As the car reached the stop sign, I thought of the intersection. It was busy after school. I got nervous thinking about Destiny sitting in the car without me to protect her—all alone. Or was it me who was all alone?

"Come on." Dawna grabbed my jacket.

"I've never been this far away from Destiny. And she's never been in a car by herself—I mean without me."

I loved my baby, but that wasn't the only reason I worried when she was away from me. It was more than that. It was like she was part of my own body, and when she was away from me I had a strange feeling that part of me was missing.

"Same Mustang, Jane. Same driver, Jane. Same car seat, Jane," Dawna laughed. "Come on. You got work to do."

"I know, I know."

We ran into the school and straight to the drama room. We were early, only a few students mingled around the room.

"The technical crew is meeting in the lunchroom. Meet you here to walk home?" Dawna said.

"Sure."

I sat on the bleachers and watched the room fill with students. Allison and Corrine came in with Vanessa.

"Jane. You made it!" Allison said. She came over and sat beside me.

"Yeah. Didn't you think I would?"

"What did you do with your baby?"

"Destiny?"

"Yeah, what did you do with Destiny?"

"Kate's babysitting. She's going to babysit every Wednesday during drama practice."

Allison hadn't known what to do about Destiny from the start. It was like Destiny sat between us. So now that Destiny wasn't there, Allison was comfortable. I could be her friend again. She dumped her bags on the floor and moved close to me.

"Great, does that mean you're going to be here every week?" she asked. "How's it been? It'll be great if you can make it. *Grease* is going to be so much fun. What part do you want?"

"I don't know. Have you seen the script yet?"

"Yeah, Vanessa showed me. Mr. Knight is going to give an outline to everyone today so we can all look at it."

Vanessa was standing by the corner of the stage talking to Corrine and a couple of the guys. But she wasn't someone who liked competition, so when she saw Allison, who she seemed to consider her new best friend, talking to me, she walked over and stood in front of us.

"Surprised to see *you* here," she said.

"Yeah?"

"What about your baby? She here too?"

"You mean Destiny?" I said. There it was again. When I had Destiny I found out there were three categories of people. There were people who called her by her name, and people who ignored she existed or called her "your baby" as if she wasn't a real person. The third category was the people who called her "your baby" as if they were naming a contagious disease or were accusing me of something. The third category had talked a lot about me, and what they had said wasn't very nice.

There weren't many people in the first category, especially when it came to teenagers. Dawna was the first friend I met. The first time Dawna saw Destiny she kneeled down and talked to her. I knew right then that Dawna was different— and that was when I realized there were the three categories. Allison was in the second category and Vanessa was in the third.

"Yeah, whatever. You're not going to bring *your baby* here are you?"

I said, "No. *Destiny* is with a babysitter—every Wednesday."

"We aren't going to practise just Wednesdays, you know," she persisted. "By the time this gets rolling we will be practising two or three times a week. Have you got a babysitter to cover that?"

"I'll find one."

I felt my back straighten, my shoulders roll back, and my lungs expand. I was beginning to notice that when I felt put down about having Destiny, I stood up.

"Come on, Allison," Vanessa said, passing a distinctly vicious look my way. "We're supposed to be organizing a bottle drive."

"Okay," Allison said. "In a minute."

Vanessa walked away with her head and nose pointing straight up.

"Jane, we have to get together and talk. I have so much to tell you." Allison hugged me and stood up.

And what would we talk about?

"Later, Jane. Got to go. You going to do the bottle drive next weekend?" she called over her shoulder as she joined Vanessa and Corrine at the front.

"Later," I responded. "Probably not," I mumbled, but Allison had turned her back by then.

Mr. Knight stood at the front with the girls. I couldn't hear what he was saying, but I watched him flailing his arms and shuffling his feet as he talked. His hair, a mass of tight curls, bobbed.

"Okay, everyone!" Mr. Knight stood in the centre of the stage. "Listen up. We have a lot to do this afternoon."

Slowly the crowd gathered around.

"Vanessa's going to hand out an outline of the major parts in the production. Read them over. Rent the movie and watch it. I want to introduce the characters so you have something to think about."

"How are we all going to be able to rent the movie? The Video Stop only has one copy." I looked around to find the person with the dumb question.

Mr. Knight rolled his eyes and said, "Get together then. Watch it at someone's house. And if you rent it, don't keep it out for a week. Bring it back so someone else can rent it.

"I'm going to go over a little history around the story and each character. If you have any questions, ask them now," Mr. Knight continued.

Vanessa worked her way through the group and passed each student an outline. She tossed one on the chair beside me, making sure she didn't look at me.

"Read the outline. Get to know a character or two. A month or so before auditions we'll put a sign-up sheet on the drama club notice board. You can sign up for your first and second choice."

"What if we only want one part and we don't have a second choice?" Vanessa asked Mr. Knight after he had described Sandy, the blond innocent-turned-vixen star of the show. "I think I'm only suitable for one part."

"Don't get stuck on one part. Remember, right now we are practise, practise, practise. I just want you to have the parts in mind while you are working on your singing, acting, and dancing. Be versatile. In the end, at the auditions, the judges will decide what part you get. They'll take into consideration your first and second choices, but they make the final decision."

When the meeting was over, Vanessa began singing, "*Summer love* . . . The only problem is, who is going to be Danny?" she called out to Allison. "I just hope he's tall enough. It has to be Mark."

Positive thinking can get you a lot. I knew that, and Vanessa knew it too. She believed she was going to get the part she wanted, and she was going to make sure everyone else thought so too. As I watched her walk through the crowd

I had to admit to myself that if the production was going to be cast like the movie, then Vanessa was the only one in the drama club who looked anything like Olivia Newton-John. I had watched the movie tons of times and I knew I, on the other hand, didn't look like any of the actors. There were no black kids in the movie—except maybe for a fleeting shot of a black boy sitting in a desk. There were no Chinese or Pakistanis or Filipinos and there were certainly no Indians. There was one Hispanic-looking girl, but I didn't look like her either.

"Let me look!" Dawna grabbed the outline when she ran back into the drama room. "What part do you want? Who are you going to be?"

"I don't know," I said while she was reading. "I guess I could go for Frenchy or Marty. There's no way I want to play Patti Simcox. And not a chance I want to be Rizzo." I didn't need to play the girl who thought she was pregnant and had a reputation for sleeping around.

The room emptied.

"Sandy." Dawna stuffed the outline into my knapsack. "You have to go for Sandy."

"No way!" I laughed. "Me? Sandy? You're crazy. You ever seen the movie?"

"Does this look like Hollywood? Yeah, I've seen the movie, and you would be great as Sandy."

"Dawna, really. Seriously, who do you think I should try out for?"

"Sandy."

"Dawna," I said, "I mean for real. Do you think I should try out for Frenchy? She has a pretty big role and she has one solo. I'd love to do a solo."

"I am for real. I think you should try out for Sandy. I hear you singing to Destiny. You have a beautiful voice, just like Olivia Newton-John."

"Vanessa looks perfect for the part. She's tall, blond, blue-eyed, her legs go on forever, she takes singing lessons, and she's been trained in dance since she was three. Look at me. I'm short. I don't reach her shoulders even when I've got heels on. I'm Indian. Since when is Sandy an Indian? What are they going to do, put a blond wig on me? I've got a baby. Sandy is innocent. She hasn't even kissed, barely."

"You don't get it. This is *theatre*. You should know that. This isn't about those things. They can cast anyone they want in the role."

"No way."

"You afraid?"

"I'm not afraid," I said. But once the words came out I knew I was afraid. I was afraid to put myself out in front of people and say I might be good enough. I was afraid of what people might say. I could hear it already—She has a baby. She shouldn't play that role. I was afraid they would want to put me off to the side where I wouldn't be too conspicuous. They wouldn't want the star to be changing a diaper during intermission.

When we walked around the corner onto Terrace Avenue a hot flush crept up my neck and behind my ears. *Is Destiny okay?* Suddenly it felt like I hadn't seen her for days. *Wonder if she fell? Wonder if she choked? Kate wouldn't have been able to call me or tell me.*

I checked the driveway for the Mustang. It wasn't there. *Has Joey taken Destiny to the hospital?*

I held my breath and ran up the path to the front door and immediately heard Kate say, "Your mommy's home, baby girl."

I ran up the stairs and picked up Destiny. "Sweet baby. You're fine!" I breathed a sigh of relief when I hugged her.

"Yeah, she's fine," Kate said, slightly offended. "Didn't you think she would be?"

"Sorry." I finally sat down. "It's the first time I've ever been that far away from her. And you can't believe it. It's crazy-making. First you want more than anything to be away from your baby. But then when she's gone you're scared that she'll die without you or that you'll die without her."

Kate picked up the stuffed kittens and teddy bears. "I had such a good time. I can't wait until next week. Get used to it. She's fine without you."

"Come on, Joey, please. You have to go to the other video stores and look for it," I begged him.

"We'll make the popcorn and buy the pop if you find the movie. We'll even make pizzas," Dawna said. "I got money."

Finally Joey agreed.

That night Joey, Kate, and Pete joined Dawna and me for a *Grease* party. We watched the movie three times.

"There you are, Jane. That's the one you should do for your audition," Dawna said when Sandy sang "Hopelessly Devoted to You."

"It's too sappy. I need to sing something upbeat. I want to dance too. I think I should be Frenchy and sing 'Beauty School Dropout'," I said. It wasn't so much that I couldn't imagine playing the part of Sandy; I just couldn't imagine anyone picking me for the part over Vanessa.

"Okay, pick Frenchy for your second choice. But you have to audition for Sandy. Who cares if Vanessa thinks she's got the part?" Dawna said.

I knew I could be Frenchy. In fact I kind of felt like Frenchy—the girl who didn't make it, the girl who dropped out of school, the girl who stood slightly over to the side of the group. Frenchy was the one who had a good heart. She would help you with anything. That was me. Vanessa was the right person for the part of Sandy. She didn't only look like her—she *was* a Sandy. Vanessa had been raised to be Sandra Dee, the perfect person—although she partied a lot more than the Sandy character in the movie. Still she walked around like she had never done anything wrong in her life. Vanessa was born to be a star. I just dreamed about being a star. I figured I would be lucky if I could just get to drama practices regularly and be one of the chorus dancers.

"You have to do it," Kate joined Dawna.

Joey agreed. "Be a star, sister. Go for it. Take it all."

"Don't let Vanessa stop you. She sucks," Pete sneered. "She doesn't have any talent—she just walks around trying to impress people. Everyone knows she's just a rich bitch. Why are you letting her intimidate you? You got more than that." Pete sounded annoyed. He got up and headed downstairs, then he turned around and said, "Way more. You got guts, Jane."

After Dawna and Kate went home I crawled into bed. I heard the faint in-and-out of Destiny's breathing. Pete and Joey had gone to bed. Dad had gone to bed. Teh was sleeping. I listened to the stillness. I thought about the last thing Mom said to me before she died . . . I thought again about Pete's words—You got guts, Jane.

I watched a white streak of moonlight stretch across the ceiling. I lay perfectly still. I felt my body without touching it. My fingernails, the tiny hairs on my fingers, my warm prickly armpits that needed to be shaved, my shoulders, strong and square. My breasts, smaller now, and my belly, soft but tighter. I imagined stroking my legs—they were long, for a short person, and fine-boned. A dancer's legs and feet—that's what my dance teacher had said in grade six.

Men wrapped in blankets brush the floor with cedar boughs and sprinkle fresh water behind them as they scurry out the back door. The dirt floor is smooth. It glistens like freshly polished oak. People crowd into the bleachers. Women hold their drumsticks high, and at the command of an invisible conductor they beat the rhythm of the heart. There are no fires. Instead, lights hang on tall metal poles. And cameras. From an opening in the roof a stage descends. On the edge of the stage a young woman curls around her legs.

8

Having Destiny in the house changed things for everybody. Pete and Joey did dishes. Not a lot of dishes, but more than they'd done probably in their whole lives. Other than the odd comment about whose turn it was and how busy they were, they didn't seem to mind. Dad stayed home some nights and held Destiny while I got my homework done. It started gradually. I noticed he was hanging around, asking me what his granddaughter was doing. One day I asked him if he wanted to hold her, and after that I started bringing her out whenever he was home, and he'd sit on his recliner with her resting on his chest until both fell asleep. Later he would tiptoe into my room and lay her on the bed. He'd kiss his finger and touch her forehead. He never said much to me, but it felt good to have him around.

Things had fallen into a jerky rhythm. Each day created a flow that made the next day easier. I fitted school, showers, and sleep around feeding, changing, rocking Destiny, and hoping she would sleep more than two hours in a row. Monday to Friday established a pattern, leaving the weekend for doing the things that got left out during the week. But there was never quite enough time for anything. I found I completed some things, like looking after Destiny. I did half of other things, like cleaning my room, cooking, and doing my homework. And I totally didn't do other things like talking on the phone, having long baths, and reading novels.

I never went out for my fifteenth birthday either, October 29. But Sunday we at least got together and had a family dinner. It lasted until I had to put Destiny to bed, and then I fell asleep. And totally forgot math.

Monday, first class, I ran from the daycare just in time to collapse in my seat as the bell rang. I shuffled as inconspicuously as possible under the glare of Mrs. Jackson's beady eyes. Her glasses were so thick they made her eyes look like telescopes, and they always seemed to be focused on me.

She said, "Jane, can't you manage to get here on time?"

Other kids wandered in behind me, but she didn't seem to notice. I had decided at the beginning of the year that the best way to deal with her was to ignore her as much as possible.

"Pull out your homework," she said. She still had her eyes peeled in my direction. "I want to go over it before we go on to a new chapter."

I had started it. I knew I had gotten some of it done Friday night. And I stuffed it in my knapsack. At least I thought I did. I rummaged through the papers, fruit, granola bars, and baby clothes and finally pulled out my binder.

The first two pages were completed. They were there somewhere.

"Jane, could you go through number one for us?"

I had that sick feeling of being trapped. The pages weren't anywhere. Not even the ones I had done.

I kept my head down, leafing through my binder.

"Jane." She stood next to my desk. "Number one."

Just then I remembered exactly where I had put the homework.

"I left my homework in the diaper bag. It's in the daycare," I said. For a moment I was relieved. "I'll just run out and get it."

Mrs. Jackson blocked my chair. I could hardly move without bumping into her.

"You forgot your homework. You won't go anywhere."

"No. It's at school, right outside. I can get it," I said. At least half of it was outside. "I know exactly how to do number one."

"The daycare is not the school, Jane," she said. "You will be here at lunch to do your homework."

She waited for me to reply.

"You'll be here at lunch, won't you." It wasn't a question. It was a demand. "Right, Jane."

"I can't come in at lunch," I mumbled. By this time the rest of the class had settled in and everyone was watching our conversation.

"Why?" She needed to rub it in.

"I have to be in the daycare."

She gasped as if she had just heard something awful. "Are you a student or are you a mother?" She turned and stomped back to the front of the class. "I don't know why they have that daycare at the school in the first place. High schools are no place to be parading girls that have babies."

There was a hush in the class. I didn't see the expression on the kids' faces because I kept my head down and waited until Mrs. Jackson carried on with the class.

I got the homework done that night and placed it neatly in my binder, ready for class.

Rock music woke me up. I found myself lying on the bed, binder under my arm, still fully clothed. Thrasher music. 2:48 a.m. It was pumping straight up the vent beside the bed from the boys' room directly underneath. When my head cleared the sleep away I heard Kate's high-pitched voice.

"You're such a loser." Her words piped through the heating system. Like a siren. "If you think I'm going to wait around for you to grow up, you're wrong."

Joey mumbled something I couldn't hear.

"Don't I-love-you-Kate me! I'm finished with that!" she screeched.

Someone cranked the stereo. But the voices only got louder.

Destiny wriggled and sobbed. Soon the noise woke her up and she started crying.

Then I heard Pete shout, "Shut the hell up, you morons. I'm trying to sleep."

"Shut up yourself, Pete!" Kate blasted. "I'm not talking to you."

Destiny wasn't going to go back to sleep so I picked her up and paced back and forth. I tried to ignore the noise, but anger welled up inside. I wanted to stay out of it, but my body wouldn't keep still. I listened to the madness streaming up to my bedroom and I thought about families in houses just like ours. White houses with green or brown or black trim and shutters, where people were sleeping peacefully. They were in their beds, in their rooms. They hadn't dropped out of school. They didn't have babies at fourteen and then pack their babies off to high school. They had supper, did their homework, watched TV. Their dads were home with their moms.

We are insane.

I listened closely and could hear Teh snoring in the next

room. I stood still for a moment and looked at Destiny. Then I put a bottle in her mouth and walked slowly downstairs.

"You guys get the hell out of my bedroom," I heard Pete say.

I stood and shivered in the dark, freezing basement outside the boys' bedroom door and asked myself if I really wanted to interfere. Finally I opened the door and watched Pete tug his blanket off his bed and wrap it around his back.

"I'm out of here. What the hell are you doing in here?" he shouted when he saw me. He's the kind of guy who uses anger as a pre-emptive strike. If he sees anger coming his way, he jumps in and acts angrier. It's his strategy. He figures that if he gets mad enough, the other person will retreat. "Let's get the whole family in on it. Where's Dad and Teh? Let's get them down here too!"

"Stop it, Pete." I had to shout too, to be heard over the music.

Kate reached over and turned off the stereo. The room was instantly silent. Then she stood, hands on her hips, straight as a Barbie doll. She was the only girl I had ever met who was actually shaped like Barbie, all arms and legs. She towered over Joey, but neither of them seemed to mind. Kate was uptight and awkward, her chin formed a right angle to the ground, and her boobs, which were a lot bigger than mine, were a little too high. They confronted you, demanded something from you when you stood in front of her. In the past we stayed out of each other's way. But since Destiny was born we had gotten close. The way she helped me out was almost like a sister. When I saw the anger and strain on Kate's face I got worried. She had an I'm-going-to-leave-this-time-for-real look on her face. I knew that was not what anyone needed. Not Joey, not me, and not Destiny. I looked from one to the other.

What had I come downstairs to do? What was I thinking?

"Go ahead. What do you want to say? Start screaming at us like you usually do," Pete said.

I didn't have any words. I usually did, just like Pete said. I looked at the clock. It was 3:00.

This is nuts. My family is crazy. Mom, I need you.

"Well? Come on, I want to get to sleep," Pete snarled. "Get it over with."

"I didn't come here to scream at you." I sat Destiny on the bed next to Pete and propped pillows around her. "This is our family, guys. It's you guys, me, and Destiny. I'm trying to make a family here so my baby grows up strong and healthy. I need your help. Who else do I have?" My voice began to wobble. "Teh is getting old and she must be tired of looking after us. Dad isn't always around. I want something good for Destiny. I want people to respect us. I want to respect us." I paused. "And what about Mom? She would be so sad to see us like this. You know it."

"Don't get talking about Mom." Pete turned away.

"I'm just saying this isn't the kind of family we were."

Joey picked up Kate's hand and began stroking her fingers.

"I have to try to make it right around here. 'Cause now there's Destiny. I'm tired of screaming and then everything just being the same old useless way." The tears were streaming down my face now.

"What do you want me to do about it?" Pete asked.

"Look at yourself," I said. "You could be so much more, you know it, Pete. You were there for me when I had Destiny. I'll never forget it."

Joey moved closer to Kate and put his arm over her shoulder. "Jane's right. It's time we got our shit together."

"Get what shit together? What's all this shit about

anyway?" Pete said, jumping to his anger strategy.

"Finish school. Or get a job," Joey said. "I'm tired of being broke and bored."

"I want to get to sleep. Are you guys going to shut up now? And get out of my bedroom?" Pete lay down and rolled over so his back was toward us.

"Hey, big brother. I love you. What about giving your niece a hug? I brought her down here to see you." I tugged on Pete's blanket.

He turned around and reached for Destiny. He straightened out her sleeper and smoothed her thick black hair. He tucked his face into her neck and tickled her until she giggled.

He whispered, "Little Destiny baby. I'm going to be there for you. Your big Uncle Pete is going to get it together. I promise."

He put Destiny on my lap and turned away.

"Thanks, Jane," Joey said.

"Yeah, thanks a lot," Kate added.

"I need you guys," I said and closed the door.

As I passed through my bedroom door I heard Dad coming up the front stairs.

"Hey, Dad," I said quietly. "How's it going?"

"What are you doing up so late?" he asked.

"What are you doing coming in so late?"

"Nothing."

"Your family needs you, Dad. Do you know that?"

"I'm sorry, Jane. I've been working a lot lately."

"Till three in the morning?"

I shut my bedroom door with a bang. I didn't want to hurt him, but I didn't want to cover for him anymore either. I heard him pace up and down the hall and linger in front of my door. I waited for him to knock, then fell asleep.

9

Long nights spent with little sleep have a way of drilling holes in you. Stuff crawls in and other stuff trickles out. Nights like that can change things. In the morning you're tired and you don't always notice right away that something has happened. Sometimes you don't know till later.

It was like that for me when I woke up after being down in the boys' room. I felt like a jigsaw puzzle with a million tiny pieces dumped on the kitchen table. But I didn't put it down directly to the night before. I sat Destiny on the bed and stuffed pillows around her. I spread her feet wide apart and balanced her round, diapered bottom. If I got it just right she looked like she was sitting on her own.

"Okay, baby, let's see how long you can sit. One, two, three, four . . . eight, nine, ten. Eeee!" Destiny rolled slowly forward until her cheek smunched on the bed.

I sat her up again and counted, "One, two . . . nine, ten, eleven." She giggled. She loved the game.

"You're the best girl." I wrapped my arms around her and hugged her tightly. "You're the smartest thing, sitting up like that." It was fun to play, to sing, to make Destiny happy.

"Jane, someone's at the door," Teh hollered from the living room. "I think it's Dawna. Go see what she wants."

The clock rolled around to 7:45. I had no idea it was so late. I hadn't done a thing since I got up except play with Destiny. That was all I wanted to do. I wanted to sit her up, count, and watch her giggle as she toppled over. I wanted to make up words and sing and dance around the bedroom, swooping and bowing.

I ran downstairs and opened the door.

"Hey, girlfriend, what's up? You need some help getting ready?" Dawna said.

"I'm not going to school today," I replied. All of a sudden going to school didn't seem like the right thing to do.

"Why not?"

"I can't. I gotta stay home," I said.

"Whoa, not so easy." Dawna stepped inside the door. "You need to talk?"

"No. I just need to stay home. I don't want to go to school."

Dawna followed me to my room.

"Watch, Dawna," I said. "Look how long Destiny can sit on her own." I propped Destiny up and pulled my hands away again. "One, two . . . ten, eleven, twelve."

"You're so smart, Destiny!" Dawna exclaimed. "When did you get so smart?"

I watched Dawna play the propping game with Destiny. It was amazing. Dawna had a look of pure enjoyment on her face. She laughed out loud and repeated the game over and over, long after most teenagers would have been bored and fed up.

I couldn't find the words, but I wanted to tell Dawna how lucky I was to have a friend like her. I wanted to say that even though we had only just met, I loved spending time with her, I needed her, and Destiny was lucky too.

Dawna was different from my other friends. She wore hiking boots, jeans with flannel shirts and jogging shoes, fleece vests and sweatshirts. We didn't talk a lot about clothes. We talked about other stuff, like music, dance, theatre, people—we talked about people a lot, and school. Regular stuff—but talking with Dawna was different too. She didn't wait for her turn while you talked—she listened. She wanted to know how you felt and how you were going to work things out. She talked about what things meant to people and how people affect other people. She didn't interrupt or finish your sentence with "Yeah, I know." Dawna read the newspaper and magazines like *National Geographic* and *Life*. She talked about what was going on in the world, how different things looked in pictures, and how she hoped to preserve animal habitat when she got older.

"Jane," Dawna exclaimed. She picked Destiny up and swung around. "She got to fourteen. That's the best yet!"

She propped her up again. "Oooooh, how long you going to sit up this time, baby?" Dawna opened her mouth and eyes wide in exclamation and clasped her temples. Destiny giggled so hard she toppled over immediately.

I knew as I watched that Destiny was sent to me, out of the blue, and so was Dawna—but that morning there were so many things I didn't know. I felt like I was passing in the fog, slippery, crossing a busy street, running to the bus, rushing through a crowd, clasping a hand.

"I can't do it, Dawna."

Destiny and Dawna giggled.

"I can't do it," I said again.

"I hear you. I hear you." Dawna sat down and looked in my eyes. "You can't do what?"

"I can't get up every morning and pack my baby away and

take off. Come home, rush around. My life is crazy. Everything is too much!"

"What's everything?"

"I have to be Destiny's mother, I have to take care of my brothers, I have to help Teh so her life isn't such a grind, and then there's Dad. I don't know what's up with him. And then I have to go to school and be in the daycare all the time. I'm so far behind on my homework—I'm barely keeping up with math. Yesterday Mrs. Jackson nailed me in class. She's twice as hard on me as anyone else!"

"Whoa," Dawna said. She flung her arms back onto the bed and lay spread-eagled.

I hardly heard her. There was more. "I should just look after Destiny. Stay home and help Teh. I shouldn't try to finish school with my friends. I can go back next year. And then there's drama. I'm out of my mind if I think I can keep up with a production. I'm going to forget it."

A knot grew in my stomach, my throat tightened, and tears streamed down my cheeks. Dawna put Destiny on a blanket on the floor and lay next to me. She rested on one elbow and stroked my hair. I felt a warm, cared-for tugging.

"You want to know what I really want, Dawna?" I waited.

"Yeah, I want to know. What do you really want?" she asked.

"I—I—I really just want to be a kid. I just want to be fifteen. I want to go to school. I want to try out for musical theatre. I want to sing and dance."

The words stabbed my chest and stung my throat as they escaped out of my mouth. Dawna drew me into her arms. I was safe.

Take a deep breath, Jane. Close your mouth. Get control. Breathe in and out until the pain eases. Who cares about what you want? It's too late for that now.

But I couldn't stop. Buckets of words spilled with tears onto Dawna's fleece vest.

"I want to go for a walk and not have to push a stroller. I want to pass people on the street and not have them look at me funny. I want to go to school and stay there—not spend half my time in the daycare. I want to go to parties. I want the guys to look at me like they used to—like I'm hot, not like I'm easy."

I kicked my feet and wrestled free from Dawna's grasp. The words hung in the air like they were printed on an overhead projector—for too long. I didn't like the sound of them and they hurt coming out, but now I felt relieved. I wasn't finished, but the next words were painless.

"I had plans, Dawna." I wiped my eyes. "I wasn't going to be like the rest of them. I was going to be a success. I was going to be the girl that sang and danced. I was going to go to university and act in the theatre. I was going to be the Williams that people looked up to. Now I'm just the girl with a baby. The girl who had the baby when she was fourteen and didn't tell anybody she was pregnant. That's all people think about me."

I looked up and saw Teh standing at the door. Her hand was placed firmly on her hip, and although her eyelids folded over the corners of her eyes and her cheeks drooped from lack of sleep, there was no mistaking the stern look on her face.

"You're not *just* the girl with a baby, Jane. You're not *just* anything. You're Jane Williams, mother of Destiny Mae Williams. And there's a difference. You're a mother and a teenager and a student and a sister and a granddaughter and a daughter. You're lots of things. We are all lots of things. All those things make us us. Each thing we take on becomes part of us—we don't become it."

She sat on the bed beside us.

"You had to grow up too fast when your mother died. Now you have to grow up even faster since Destiny was born. But you're doing a great job. It's a hard thing, growing up. I've never seen a young person grow up yet where it wasn't real hard."

Maybe Teh was right. But everyone else's life was beginning to look a whole lot easier than mine. Wasn't being a teenager supposed to be spontaneous, carefree, and fun?

As if reading my mind, Teh corrected me. "I don't want you going around feeling sorry for yourself. Everyone has their bucket of junk to carry, and some people's bucket looks light compared to ours. But don't you be thinking you're the only one that's got it hard in this life. Now give me my great-granddaughter and let me look after her while you two girls look after you. I don't want to see you girls going to school until lunch."

"Wow, you've got an awesome grandmother," Dawna said when Teh left with Destiny. She took off her coat and rolled up her sleeves. "Your family is amazing, Jane. The way they look after each other."

My family is amazing.

Amazing? Crazy, maybe. And definitely crazy-making. But not amazing. But we did look after each other. At least Teh and I looked after everyone else. I followed Dawna, still talking, into the bathroom. She said, "Like Joey, the way he drives you to school, and your Uncle Kenny, how he drives Teh around all the time—and Kate, the way she helps out with Destiny." Dawna turned on a hot bath and poured dollops of lavender-scented bubble bath into the water. "My family's not like that. We just ignore each other."

She tested the water.

"Did you have a hard night last night?"

"Yeah, I'll tell you about it later."

"Climb in," Dawna said as she left the bathroom. "It's all yours."

I buried myself in the soapy water and soaked. It felt like I was at an expensive spa. I shaved my legs—right up to the top—and my armpits. After I rinsed, I rubbed my skin till it tingled.

Then I took a good look at myself. My stomach was thinner than before, but it had a little loose skin that felt like pull taffy when I pulled it out. My body felt softer than before. And I noticed a few other changes in my body as I twisted and turned in front of the mirror. My breasts were larger and my butt was flatter. I reached both hands to the ceiling and felt a new suppleness I had never experienced. I bent over and spread both hands flat on the floor. Having a baby had loosened me up. I felt new, alive, as if the bath washed off a layer of scum, removed a cocoon, drew back the curtains to a brand new day.

I plucked my eyebrows and put on my makeup. Then we rummaged through my clothes until we found the perfect jeans and T-shirt. After Dawna pulled my hair up, she spiked the ends, and then I paraded around the room as if I was walking the catwalk.

"Gorgeous," Dawna exclaimed.

I swiveled my hips.

"Hot!"

"Then we're ready to go," I laughed. "It's been a long time since anyone said I was hot. It's only you, girlfriend, but hey, I'll take it."

Giddy felt good. I was just a silly teenager. My body was mine again. By the time we wrapped Destiny in her blankets and placed her in her stroller, it was almost lunchtime.

"You're beautiful, Jane," Dawna said when we walked up the road. "You sure don't look like a girl who just had a baby a few months ago."

"Thanks, Dawna."

When we reached the school, Dawna headed inside and I carried on through the parking lot. I opened the door to the daycare and was met by Karen, wiping her hands on her apron.

"I'm cooking up lunch for the kids," she said.

"Smells good," I said. Macaroni and cheese. I was starving. "Lucky kids. Sorry I'm late. I just couldn't get it together this morning."

"You could stay and have some lunch. Too bad you're busy."

I felt confused. What was she talking about?

"Your grandmother called and said that you were busy at lunch. That you wouldn't be able to stay and look after Destiny . . . something about your drama class?" Karen said, also looking a little confused.

"My drama class? Oh, yeah. Yeah. I'm sure glad she phoned. Is it okay?" I said.

"Sure. But don't make a habit of it."

"Of course not." I kissed Destiny on the forehead. "See you after school, baby girl."

I walked across the parking lot toward the school and for a few moments I felt free and wonderful. When I realized I hadn't been in the school at lunch once since the beginning of the year, the wonderful feeling turned to awkward and worried. What do normal people do at lunch? Dawna usually came into the daycare and ate with Destiny and me. We played in the daycare or walked around outside for a few minutes. I didn't even know where Dawna would be at lunch, or what I should do.

The lunch bell rang as I entered the school. Kids poured out of the classrooms and met in groups in the hall. Everyone was talking to someone. I looked around for Dawna.

"Hey!" Dawna called as she saw me wandering up the hall. "What are you doing? You lost?"

"Wow, am I glad to see you. I don't know what to do in here at lunch," I said. "Teh phoned and told Karen I was busy and that I wouldn't be able to be in the daycare. So I'm free."

"Holy," Dawna said. "Let's go buy lunch."

Kids chattered, flirted, pushed, and shoved in the cafeteria lineup. I felt like an old woman remembering back to her childhood or a little girl trying to figure out what to do.

"Jane," Allison called to me as she passed, "what have you done to yourself?"

I laughed.

"Maybe I should brush my hair more often, eh, Dawna? Did I look that bad?"

I picked up my pizza slice, Coke, and apple and sat down next to Dawna at an empty table.

"Jane."

"Jane, baby."

"Wow, Jane, long time no see."

Jason, Levi, and Thorton gathered around our table.

"Hi, guys," I said. "I haven't seen you forever."

"Yeah," Thorton said. "How've you been?"

"Good, yeah, I've been good. What about you?"

"Good, yeah. We've been good." Thorton shifted uneasily from one foot to the other. Jason and Levi stood behind him, nodding uneasily.

I felt self-conscious and on display, but mostly I felt sorry for the guys, Trevor's old buddies. They were so embarrassed. I wanted to put a stop to the small talk, to jump back in time to when we were best friends, comfortable with each other, hanging out, laughing, and joking. Now the big thing hung between us like a dead rat. Who was going to go near it?

"Hey, you guys, did you hear? I had a baby," I blurted out, trying to lighten the conversation up a bit. But the words sort of dripped for a second.

Dumb. Really dumb thing to say, Jane.

We all forced a laugh.

"Yeah, I didn't know what we were supposed to say. I guess congratulations are in order." Levi stepped forward and threw his arms around me. "Congratulations."

"Thanks, Levi."

"I hear she is a cutie." Jason loosened up and hugged me next. "Allison says she looks just like her mom."

Thorton was next. "Heard from Trevor?" he asked.

"Not since he left," I said. "Have you?"

"No, I guess he's busy in Winnipeg. He's sort of a loser." Thorton kicked the chair. "He shouldn't have left you with a baby. And then never call."

"I'm okay, Thor," I said.

"If you ever need anything . . ." His voice trailed off. He might have been thinking, like me, of what he could do for me and my baby.

"Thanks, Thor. Come over sometime. She's got Trev's eyes and she's still really cute," I said. "You guys know Dawna?"

I did a round of introductions.

"Trevor's friends," I told Dawna when the guys left. "Used to hang out with them every day. That was the weirdest thing. Sure glad we finally broke the ice."

10

Who would think that walking up and down the school halls could make you feel like you had been cured? Like you could see after your vision was blurry, like you could breathe easily after your throat was swollen, or like you could think straight after you had had a bad headache. Kids gathered in groups near water fountains, lockers, and corners. Dawna and I edged our way through the crowds.

"That was great, what Teh did for you. Telling Karen you needed a lunch off," Dawna said.

"Teh has an instinct for detecting when people need something. And she always knows how to apply a simple remedy," I said. "She says it's her medicine."

"Medicine?" Dawna asked.

"She says we're all medicine for each other. You're my medicine. I hope I'm your medicine too."

"What do you mean?"

"You're there when I need someone. You help me out and then I feel better. That's medicine."

"You're my medicine too, then. 'Cause when I got to this school I needed a friend and I found one," she said. "So we're medicine. Is that how it goes?"

"Yep. Ask Teh. We're good medicine."

I had watched Teh work her medicine for years, especially at the old house. A steady stream of friends and neighbours showed up at the door. Everyone got a cup of tea, some she invited to Bingo or gave a head massage, some she sympathized with, others she scolded, but they kept coming back. I could feel Teh's medicine working as I walked down the hall. I was a kid again, thanks to her.

Vanessa walked past us, looked over her shoulder at me, and said, "I thought *you* were supposed to be in the daycare at lunch."

I ignored her and kept walking.

"Wow, what's up with her?" Dawna said. "She sure has got it in for you. You guys got some history?"

"I guess she thinks we do," I said. "I'll tell you about it sometime. It's pretty stupid and I don't want to spoil my lunch. Let's check out the drama room."

The drama room was full of kids standing around and sitting in the bleachers. We found a free spot and sat down. Jason was there, shoulder to shoulder with Neil, Mark, and Tyrell in a line across the stage, hands resting on their hips. They looked like they were waiting impatiently for a bus or for their girlfriend to get out of the washroom, except that they had bare feet.

"Swivel," Mrs. Trenton called out. "Isolate your hips." She faced them, back to the crowd, hands on her hips. She looked just as impatient as they did, even from behind. "It doesn't matter if you're not trying out for Danny—everyone in this production has to be prepared to dance."

The guys jerked their legs and torsos and tossed their shoulders, arms, and necks into a contorted corkscrew.

"No, no," Mrs. Trenton cried with exasperation. She threw

her hands in the air. "Just your hips, not your neck and shoulders and back. You guys are going to need a chiropractor after this. I said isolate your hips. That means *just* your hips. Like this." Her thin hips snapped from side to side.

Before Mrs. Trenton became a teacher she was an award-winning ballet dancer. Her office was cluttered with trophies and ribbons from past competitions and performances. She wasn't young anymore, but she was still lithe and moved like a dancer. She could still do amazing pirouettes and pliés. But she couldn't swivel. She couldn't do the Latin thing with her hips.

She looked hilarious. Kids snickered and giggled.

"Okay, okay. So I can't do it so good either," Mrs. Trenton said and laughed. "This isn't rugby and it's not ballet and it's not working."

When they all settled down she turned to the crowd and said, "Anyone think they can show these jolting jocks how to move?"

She looked from one student to the other. Vanessa moved into Mrs. Trenton's view, waved her hand, and bounced slightly up and down. I thought Mrs. Trenton would call out Vanessa's name, but her gaze carried on past Vanessa and landed right on me.

"Jane." She pointed her finger at me and said, "You know how to swivel."

I curled my finger at my chest in amazement and dropped my jaw in shock.

"Yes, you, Jane," she said. "You can dance the tango and the salsa better than anyone. Come on up here and show these guys how to isolate."

It felt like a hundred pairs of eyes turned and stared at me.

I said, "You want *me* to show these guys how to move?"

"Yeah, come on up," she said. "Give it a try. You can't do any worse than I'm doing."

I stood up slowly, walked toward the stage and up the steps. My forward motion didn't feel like it was coming from me. Something was pushing me from behind or pulling me from in front. When I reached the centre of the stage in front of the four would-be dancers, I stopped and looked at them for a few moments. My mind was blank and my limbs were soggy. It felt like I had gone swimming in my jeans and I was dragging my legs out of the water. I shuffled a little to loosen up, hoping something would spring to mind. Nothing did.

"Music?" I asked.

I turned my back to the guys. I threw my hips back, widened my stand, and placed my hands on either side of my waist. I listened to the beat. All of a sudden something turned on—automatic pilot.

I felt like warm caramel was poured over my skin. I was smooth and supple. I hadn't danced, not really danced and felt good about it, for almost a year. But my body took over. It remembered. Slowly I moved my hands down over each hip, gently rolling them from side to side. The noise and commotion I heard from the bleachers filtered away. I rotated slowly.

For a second I forgot about the guys. When I remembered, I swung my head over my shoulder. They were standing frozen.

"Feeling, guys—loose. Follow me. Hands on your hips," I said.

Slower this time and more deliberately I caressed my hips while they swiveled—looser than ever before.

The guys started to giggle. Not laugh. They giggled that what-am-I-going-to-do-with-myself kind of giggle.

I looked straight ahead and called out to them, "Come

on. It can work. Forget the audience. Forget yourself and let it happen. Get into the feeling. Let your hips do the work."

Blood flowed warm through my body. I felt a power surge from the light directly above me. Energy struck my head, flowed through to my fingers and hands, my toes and feet, then flowed back, liquid spreading into my whole body. My hips circled left and then right. Effortlessly my body aligned with my inner rhythm. My body moved while my mind imagined.

An amphitheatre. Not in Rome or Greece. Somewhere close to the home of the small Indian girl who crouches, curled in to her ankles at the centre of the round stage. Only hushed shuffles and murmurs can be heard above the Latin rhythm. The music mounts and reverberates. The girl's bones vibrate. Her limbs remain entwined until she thinks the music will slit her open and cause her to burst onto the crowd. Instead she swallows the tension and unfolds slowly, as if pulling against herself. Buckskin is wrapped tightly over her breasts and belly and round hips, freeing itself in tassels and beads and shells over her copper shoulders and knees. Her ankles are bound with deer-hoof collars and her hair tied in leather and feathers. She raises her hands to the sky.

And dances the dance of the maiden, the rock star, the bear, the mother, the transformer. She quivers and turns until she expands and fills the theatre. There is only room for her and the applause.

Oddly in the distance I heard "Hey" and "Yeah" coming from the guys. Soon the audience and Mrs. Trenton began to clap and cheer. After a few minutes I looked over my shoulder. The guys weren't giggling anymore. They were concentrating on my hips and synchronizing their sinewy limbs and torsos with my rhythm. You wouldn't say that they were completely isolating their hips. They weren't swiveling in any way like

John Travolta. But they were onto it. They were fluid. They were warm.

When the music stopped we got a standing ovation. Wild cheers, whistles, and ooh-la-la's spread through the theatre. I wished I could have seen what was going on behind me, but from the response I could tell it must have been pretty good. The guys gathered around me, congratulating themselves on how great they were.

"Thanks for the moves, Jane," they said.

"I didn't know I had such great hips," Mark said. "Look out for the Latin lover."

"Thank you, Jane," Mrs. Trenton said and hopped up on the stage. "You were good, guys. All of you." She turned to me and said, "And you—my god, you were great. Do you think you could come in during lunch hours and help me out with these guys?"

Vanessa had followed the teacher up the stairs and listened to the conversation. "I would *love* to help with the guys," she interrupted. "*I'm* free at lunch."

"Jane," Mrs. Trenton said. She didn't seem to notice Vanessa. "Are you free tomorrow?" She laughed. "You worked wonders. I saw some isolation. There were moments when the guys showed some real swivel."

"Jane's in the daycare at lunch," Vanessa said. She elbowed her way in front of me. "Jane has a baby and isn't available. I can swivel my hips. Loretta, my jazz instructor, says I'm the best she's ever seen."

Vanessa was the girl in the school who probably everyone would say had class. You could tell just by looking at her that she had pretty much everything a girl could have. She had had dance lessons, swimming lessons, horseback riding lessons. Since she was little she had had her hair done, her nails done, her body done, deportment classes—I think that's what they were called. She'd traveled to exotic countries. She'd learned foreign languages, to play the violin, and to sing, and when the Governor General or an important author or musician came to town, Vanessa's family would have them over for dinner. Vanessa had too much going for her to have to embarrass herself in order to get what she wanted. So it was surprising to watch her interrupt Mrs. Trenton the way she did that day.

Mrs. Trenton raised an eyebrow. I peeked around from behind Vanessa.

"I'd love to help," I said. "The daycare supervisor may be able to let me out for a few lunch hours. I'll get back to you on that."

Mrs. Trenton said, "Great. And don't forget, Jane, in case you didn't hear, Mr. Knight is putting the sign-up sheets on the notice board tomorrow morning. It's early, I know, but he wants to give everyone enough time to prepare a great audition for the part they want."

Before Mrs. Trenton finished, Vanessa stomped off. Her eyes were red and watery—she looked desperate and angry. I could tell what she thought. It wasn't just a few lunchtime lessons. It meant my foot was edging in the door of the role that she had already decided was hers. Teachers were watching and she wanted them watching her, not me.

"Okay," Dawna said as we left the drama room, heading toward our lockers. "That girl sure looked like a dunce. Now you *definitely* have to try out for Sandy. I don't care how many lessons she's had—there's no way she could swivel better than you. You should have seen the guys' faces!"

"It felt so good, Dawna. I love it. I love it. I love it. Pure exhilaration. Like flying or skydiving or racing a horse.

Ecstasy," I exclaimed. Then I said seriously, "But I can't do it every lunchtime. You know I can't. I'm going to have to tell Mrs. Trenton."

After a long and thoughtful pause Dawna said, "How about if I take your place in the daycare a few times? Will Karen go for that?"

"No. I can't let you do that," I replied. I didn't want to even think about it. But "No" was never a good answer for Dawna, even if it was the right one.

"I don't mind," she said. "I don't have much to do at lunch anyway. I don't know anyone around here except you and Destiny."

I hadn't noticed before Dawna said it, but school had become just the two of us and Destiny. Allison was still my friend, but she wasn't there anymore, not for hanging around.

The bell rang and we hurried toward the classroom.

"No, Dawna," I repeated. "I can't let you cover for me like that. It's me that had the baby."

"Yeah, it's you. I know that. But Destiny's my friend too, you know. What if I want to spend some time with Destiny?" She laughed. She would find a way, if she could, to win this one. She changed the subject. "How did your Teh know that there was something you needed to do in the drama room?"

"You don't know my Teh, Dawna. I can never tell if she knows that stuff is going to happen or whether she makes stuff happen. But she had it right on. And I'm glad she did. It was pretty good medicine she dished out today," I said.

"That's her over there."

"The girl with the baby."

"You should have seen her at lunch teaching the guys how to swivel their hips."

"They were drooling."

"She was great. She doesn't look like she had a baby."

I tried not to hear, but whispers floated and swirled like sand in a windstorm.

"Teh." I stumbled in the front door, dropped my stuff, and threw my arms around her.

"How did you make out at lunch today, Jane? Okay?" Teh said. Her eyes sparkled. She rubbed her dewy cheek against my face.

"Teh, it was the greatest. And you already knew." I watched her face closely to check out her response. "You knew, didn't you?"

"What did I know, Granddaughter? I knew you needed a lunch hour to yourself. I knew you needed to work with your drama class." Teh began to laugh. "Now you tell me what I don't know. What happened in that drama room today at lunch?"

She picked up Destiny and I told her the whole story.

"And Teh," I said when I finished, "you can't believe what I felt like when I was on the stage. I was free. I was transformed. Beautiful images swelled up inside me. It's the most wonderful feeling in the world. My body and spirit come alive."

Teh began to dance around the kitchen with Destiny. She lifted her skirt and swiveled her hips.

"Oh, stop it, Teh," I cried.

"You got it all from your grandmother, Jane. Can't you see it?"

Soon we were twirling and shimmying through the house,

this time to Teh's favourite music—country twang.

I'm a slower longer kind of woman . . .

"That's me," she cooed.

. . . you say let's go baby . . . you say let's go faster harder baby . . . but I say I'm a slower longer kind of woman.

11

The next morning I couldn't get ready fast enough. I dressed Destiny and rushed around the kitchen filling her bottles.

"What's going on with you this morning?" Teh asked. She shuffled over to the coffee maker and poured herself a cup.

I opened a can of formula and diluted it with tap water.

"I don't want to be late. If Joey doesn't get up soon, I'm walking to school."

"Granddaughter," Teh said, "do you have a minute for Teh this morning? You can't be in that much of a hurry."

I followed her into the living room and plopped onto the sofa beside her rocker.

"I'll give Joey a few more minutes," I said.

"Okay, okay. Give him a few minutes. What's the hurry?"

Teh didn't usually pry into my life. But since I hadn't told her or anyone about being pregnant, she had become unusually suspicious about me. She kept her eye on me, hoping to observe the tiniest shifts in behaviour, just in case I was not telling her something. "You're as light as a dry leaf fluttering around, hurrying and scurrying." Teh closed her eyes and took a long slurp of her coffee, followed by a deeply satisfied *Ahhhhh.* "What's up?"

If something had happened I would have known what to say right away. But it wasn't like I had fallen in love or won a contest. I only knew that this day wasn't like the one before. Sometimes my life was like a maze. I would head one way and then another. I would walk back and forth over the same place, bumping into the same walls and turning around the same corners. Sometimes I didn't know what I was doing. I only had a muddled feeling and I wasn't sure how to straighten it out. But once in awhile life aligned itself. I could see ahead and side to side. When I breathed in I knew the oxygen had gotten to my lungs. When I took a step I knew I was going to get ahead.

"Well, Teh. Yesterday I didn't know what I was going to do. Today I do," I said.

"And what's that?"

"Well, Mr. Knight's posting the sign-up sheets on the notice board this morning."

"And what has that got to do with your hurry?" Teh asked.

"I'm going to audition for the part of Sandy. I'm going to put my name on the list—first choice Sandy, second choice Frenchy. I mean it. I'm going to get the part, and if I don't it doesn't matter."

"That's exactly what you should do." Teh nodded at her coffee. "Just think—our Jane." She thought for a moment. "I wish your mom could see you—the star of the show."

"Not exactly, Teh," I said. "At least, not yet."

"If you want the lead role, girl, then you go get the lead role," Teh said.

As far as Teh was concerned, I already had the part. She supported me in almost anything. Like when I was five, and she helped me make lemonade and set up a stand outside her house. We nailed a sign on the tree—five cents a glass. I made twenty-five cents all day, and it cost Teh more than that to buy the juice. But I remembered her being so excited when I came into the house at the end of the day carrying a handful of nickels. Teh was right behind me when I was eight and entered the community talent contest. She bought me a baton and dressed me up in a red, white, and blue tutu. I looked like a little American poster girl strutting across the stage. The only time Teh didn't support me was last summer when Allison and Corrine wanted me to go bungee jumping with them. "You think I'm going to sign a paper to say my granddaughter can jump off a bridge head down into a ravine, hooked by a bit of rope?" she had said. "I don't think so."

"I'm up against really stiff competition from at least one person," I said.

"The more competition the better. It makes you try harder," Teh reassured me.

"But Vanessa—that's the other girl who's trying out for Sandy—she's a trained dancer and a trained singer. And it doesn't hurt that she looks just like the actress from the movie."

"Don't let that get in your way. There's already been one tall, blond, blue-eyed Sandy. It's time for a raven-haired, chocolate-eyed Sandy," Teh said. "With braids," she added and laughed.

"Yeah, right, Teh." I laughed too. "The real problem is that the part of Sandy in the movie is such an innocent. And I have a baby."

"It's theatre, not real life. And where is all that confidence I've been seeing this morning?" Teh caressed her cup. "You've made the right decision, Jane. Stick to it."

"Thanks, Teh. I'm going to school right now to sign my

name on the sheet. Then I won't be able to change my mind."
I threw my arms around Teh and hugged her.

In spite of the clear sky and bright sun it was freezing. I met Dawna on her way to our house and we walked briskly up the road to stay warm. Destiny looked like a snowman, bundled in a white snowsuit, mitts, toque, and blankets. Her nose and cheeks shone like freshly waxed Macintosh apples.

"So, Jane," Dawna said when we entered the parking lot. "Early sign-up. Are you ready? Have you decided?"

"Sure have. And you can wait to find out," I said, teasing her. After we dropped Destiny off at the daycare we ran into the school and straight to the notice board. A few girls were signing their names, so we waited until they finished. Then I wrote my name in the "Second Choice" column next to "Frenchy." And in bold letters I wrote JANE next to "Sandy" in the "First Choice" column, directly under Vanessa's name, the only one already there. I checked the list for Vanessa's second choice, but her name appeared only once.

"Come on, let me see." Dawna pushed me aside and checked the list. "Yeah! You're going to do it." Then she looked more carefully. "Wow, Vanessa is sure confident of herself."

The bell rang.

"And that's going to be too bad for her because I know who's going to get the leading role." Dawna punched my arm playfully. "And that's you."

Before I went to the daycare at lunch I went looking for Jason. He was the only guy I could think of who could help me.

"I need you to sing the male part for my audition," I told him. "I'll be Sandy and you can be Danny."

"No way, man. I can't sing," Jason said.

"I'll practise with you. You don't have to be great," I said. "I'll give you extra dance lessons if you help me out." I couldn't give up. I needed someone. Since I talked to him in the cafeteria and we broke the ice about Destiny it looked like we could be friends again. "What part do you want?"

"Kenickie," Jason replied.

"Then you're going to need some dance lessons. And singing lessons too. Come on, Jason, please."

After a pause he said, "I'll think about it."

"Thank you so much, you're great."

"I said I'd think about it," he laughed. "Are you sure you want to try out for Sandy? I heard that Vanessa has it wrapped up."

"Where did you hear that?" I asked.

"Everyone is saying it. I didn't even know you were trying out for it."

"I signed up this morning before class. Don't you think I have a chance?"

"I'm not saying that. It's just that Vanessa always gets what she wants. You know that," he said.

"Tell me for real. Do you think I should try for it?"

"Yeah. You have a chance. And I think I *am* going to help you out with it. I'm pretty sick of her attitude."

"We can practise together. I'll help you out with Kenickie. And you can help me out with Sandy."

"Okay." Jason nodded. "Sure, I'm going to need the practice anyway. But you can't laugh at me."

It didn't take long for the news to get around that I was challenging Vanessa for the leading role. Of course people said *I* was challenging *her*, not the other way around, and it wasn't just because Vanessa's name was first on the list. No one could believe I was even trying.

When I saw Allison a few days later she shouted, "Hey, Jane! Long time no see. I heard you're trying out for the lead role."

"Yeah," I replied.

"Vanessa is furious. She said Sandy is her part and everyone should have known that. She said she's worked hard for the drama club and she thinks that she's the only one who deserves that role," Allison said.

I listened closely and watched the expression on Allison's face. Was that what Vanessa thought or what Allison thought as well? "Mr. Knight said that each part will go to whoever is the best," I said. "I don't think being the president of the drama club and organizing bottle drives means you should get whatever part you want. Or even if her father donates piles of money. She's going to have to try out just like everyone else."

"Oh, man, I'd really feel bad for her if she didn't get it. She's going to take private acting lessons just for the audition. She says it's either Sandy or nothing," Allison said. So that was it—even Allison wanted Vanessa to get the part. "Anyway, if you don't get to be Sandy you could be Frenchy or Rizzo."

Her words stung on my skin. *She deserves it. She's worked so hard for the drama club.* Of course everyone thought she deserved it. I didn't even know if I could get out to all the practices.

All of a sudden I felt the confidence I'd had for the past few days slipping. It was like I was sitting in a hot tub and someone pulled the plug. I was left high and dry with myself . . .

I could feel the drain sucking the water from under my feet. I was left wondering what I was doing—whether I had made the right decision or not. When Allison turned and walked away, part of me wanted to run after her and tell her how stupid it was of me to even think of being in the lead role, that really all I wanted to do was dance in the chorus. Another part of me wanted to cry. How could Allison support Vanessa and not me? We were best friends—at least we used to be. Another part of me got angry.

"I can do it," I said. "I'll show you I can do it."

But she didn't hear me. She had already walked out of sight.

"And anyway, it's too late. I've already signed my name and everyone is talking. I can't back out now," I said out loud to no one in particular.

"Dawna," I said as we packed up Destiny that day after school, "what have I got myself into? Even Allison thinks Vanessa should get the lead."

"Not everyone is on her side," Dawna replied. "Jason wasn't."

"I know. That's pretty great, eh?" I said. "But . . . it's not the role so much. I just want to try out for it. To see how good I can be."

"How *great* you can be," Dawna added.

"I should have known everyone would be talking," I said.

"So? It's simple," said Dawna, shrugging. "Don't listen. Just do what you're going to do."

I felt my confidence return. "Thanks. I will."

Teh was busy in the kitchen when Destiny and I got home. Teh's cleaning didn't involve much more than stacking things in piles around the edges of rooms, on stairs and shelves, and on top of and under tables and chairs. But she liked cooking. When it was my job, meals usually consisted of make-your-own submarine sandwiches, macaroni and cheese, spaghetti or other pasta with sauce from a tin. Teh cooked from scratch. Fish and potatoes, spaghetti and meatballs, clam chowder, hamburger stew, fried oysters sometimes, and crabs, if we were lucky. And fried bread. Teh made the best fried bread.

When she'd prepare a meal she wanted everyone there to eat it. We would all have to sit down at the table for supper together. Me at one end, Dad at the other, and Teh and the boys on either side. For Destiny and me, supper wasn't always convenient. Teh's call might interrupt Destiny's feeding or bathing. Sometimes I was in the middle of my homework, or Destiny was sleeping. But I didn't want to hurt Teh's feelings, so I usually stuffed a soother into Destiny's mouth, ran to the table, and sat down. One hand held Destiny, one hand held my fork.

Supper was the time that Teh would let us know what was going on, like Auntie Judy bought *another* new car or Uncle Travis is running for chief *for the third time* or the chief of the Assembly of First Nations is complaining *again, when* is he going to start talking positive? Teh had drawn her own line between gossip and news, and she made sure she never crossed it. But she always had a slant on her stories and she added her emphasis without apology. Teh believed in sharing information and what she thought of it. If Pete or Joey complained about her stories she would say, "How else are we going to stick together if we don't know about each other? We'll all become strangers. It's time you young people started thinking about what's going on in the world."

That night we barely had time to sit down before Teh

announced, "We're having Boxing Day dinner at our house this year."

The room was quiet except for the clinking and scraping of forks and spoons. Everyone was too busy serving themselves spaghetti to respond to her announcement.

"Auntie Mary's coming over from the States," she continued. "She's going to give her Indian name to Destiny— Say woo see wa. Pete, you need to wash that cap."

"Yeah." Pete slathered butter on fried bread and munched with firm concentration. He didn't like talking at meals. He liked eating. You could tell by looking at him. He wasn't fat, but if you walked by him when the light was thin, his silhouette was massive, like he was wearing a down winter jacket. It ran in the family, Teh said—the Williams are all thick and stocky, and Pete was even taller and bulkier than most.

"Say woo see wa," Teh repeated by way of getting back to telling about Auntie Mary and the naming. "It was my mother's and my grandmother's name." Teh looked at me. "You're lucky she has chosen your daughter to carry it. Auntie Mary's coming over on Boxing Day to make the arrangements for the gathering."

"She wants to give her name to Destiny?" I asked. I was surprised. "First I've heard of it. When does she want to do it? The naming?"

Teh and I dominated most supper conversations. We would gladly have let the others talk, but they mostly just grunted or mumbled a "pass the potatoes."

"She wants the naming at the end of March. Here at the bighouse. Auntie Mary isn't feeling so good these days. She figures she isn't going to live long. Mind you, she's been saying that since before you were born. But she wants to make sure she is around to pass on her name."

"No way," Pete blurted out. "End of March? That's not enough time to get the stuff together."

Naming ceremonies are big events, and the biggest part of it all is collecting gifts for everyone who attends. Usually the family prepared for months, even years, in advance. And always they cost a lot of money.

"How come Destiny is going to get her name?" I asked. Say woo see wa was an important name. I had heard a lot of stories about the old women in the family who carried that name. Great-Great-Say woo see wa traveled south into the States with her six children after her husband died of a fever. She moved her family from field to field as the crops ripened. She picked berries, corn, hops, apples, and then finally potatoes before she returned home with just enough money to fix up their shack for the winter.

I had seen the beautiful sweaters Great-Say woo see wa knit. Teh told us about her mom working for weeks preparing the wool and then sitting up late at night knitting sweater after sweater. Once she finished four or five she'd wrap them in a blanket and pack them into the canoe. Then she paddled to town where she sold them for enough money to buy shoes and clothes from the second-hand, and groceries for the week. "When there was no work for Dad," Teh had explained, "or when his drinking got too bad, Mom's knitting money was all we had to depend on." Teh's mother decided before she died that the name should go to Auntie Mary, and now Auntie was giving the name back to our side of the family. Sometimes it got complicated, but the old people never got mixed up. Names were something the family kept track of.

"Everyone thought her Esther would get it," Teh answered my question. "But Auntie Mary said Esther couldn't carry a name like that, not with all her partying and carrying on.

She phoned me today and told me. I had no idea. Mary said she's waited long enough to see if Esther would shape up and she won't wait any longer. The name can't be buried with her."

"But why Destiny?" I asked.

"She says she has watched you since you were a little girl and she knew you were the one in the family who showed the strength and power of the old women. She said Destiny will be brought up with respect. She'll be educated and she'll be smart in the old ways and in the new ways. She wants the name to be worn by somebody who will honour it."

Wow. "That's amazing."

I couldn't believe Destiny would be the next Say woo see wa. It was exciting, but at the same time it felt like a heavy responsibility. I knew the family would keep their eyes on me to make sure I appreciated the name and that I raised Destiny in a way that honoured it.

All I need is more eyes on me—something more to live up to.

"And now she wants us to put on a naming in, what—four months?" Pete said. You could tell he was thinking about what that was going to mean to him, all the stuff he was going to be expected to do.

"No need to be like that," Teh said. "She's putting it on and the whole family will help out."

I got to thinking like Pete. The end of March was right in the middle of rehearsals. The final production would take place only a few weeks later. If I did get the part of Sandy I would be too busy to help with the naming ceremony. I couldn't miss rehearsals. There was going to be too much to do.

"Does that mean the whole family's coming?" Dad mumbled.

"As many as can make it." Teh lowered her eyebrow as if

she was mentally tabulating how many she'd have to cook Boxing Day dinner for—twenty or thirty depending on how many children came.

12

I picked up the scattered *Hot Rod* and *Wrestling* magazines from the family room floor, threw the beer cans and pop bottles into an empty case, and tossed the taco chip bags into the garbage. I stacked the blankets Teh had already pulled out of the closets for the naming behind the sofa just before the doorbell rang.

I flew up the stairs and opened the door.

"Come in," I said with a twinge of discomfort in the back of my throat.

Jason moved past me into the foyer. "Hi."

Hurry up, Dawna. You were supposed to be here before Jason arrived.

"Come on downstairs," I said as I led him toward the basement.

It was a good idea, getting him over and practising our parts. But I hadn't really thought about how it was all going to work out. Jason had been one of Trevor's best friends, he'd dated Vanessa, and he'd been my friend, but never just him and me. Now we were alone in the basement.

"We can practise in here." I walked into the family room.

"I have the music script from the band class and photocopied one for you."

"How are we going to do this?" Jason looked blank-faced at the music. "I don't know how to read music. And I don't know how to sing."

I had practised "Summer Nights" every day since I signed my name beside "Sandy" the week before. I had sung it in the shower and to Destiny when she went to sleep, when she woke up, when she ate breakfast. I had even dragged Pete, Joey, and Kate into the living room, sat them on the sofa, and performed. The whole song.

"Wow," Pete had said. "I didn't know you were so great, Jane. You can really sing."

His response had made me feel strong, like I could do it. But now I forgot all my plans for how Jason and I would practise together. Now that we were sitting in the family room, looking blankly at the script, I forgot.

Jason wasn't the best-looking guy in the school. He wasn't hot. Not like Mark, his best friend, who was trying out for the lead, Danny Zuko. The thing about Jason was his eyes. When he looked up from the script I had an impulse to fix my hair or straighten my shirt. He seemed to be looking at something in particular.

The other thing about Jason was his confidence. I used to think he was arrogant, even snotty. It was the way he walked down the hall, usually in a pair of shorts and a T-shirt with some kind of ball under his arm. He played soccer, rugby, basketball, anything. And he was good, one of the best at whatever sport he played. Once I got to know him a little better I realized he had the quality I liked most in people. He had a sense of himself, the sense that gives people the right to say yes or say no. To agree or disagree. As he sat on the torn arm of the old sofa, fumbling with the script, I sensed he was as uncomfortable as I was. It was unusual and it threw me.

I figured I had gotten us into this and I better take control.

"I was thinking that we could sing 'Summer Nights' together," I said, a little unsure. "I've worked out a simple choreography we can use while we're singing."

God, when is Dawna coming? This is too damn weird.

"Are we just going to sing here, tonight? Like, together?" Jason looked almost terrified.

"Yeah," I said. "Not such a good idea? Don't you want to?"

Just as the tension reached a peak and you could have bathed in the sweat in my armpits, Kate opened the door and walked in carrying Destiny.

"Sorry for interrupting." She passed Destiny to me. "I just brought Destiny down to kiss her mommy goodnight."

Mommy! Kiss Mommy goodnight! Right here when Jason's looking!

I took Destiny stiffly.

"Goodnight, baby." I held her like my limbs were made of bamboo and kissed her quickly. As I hurried to pass her back to Kate, Destiny grabbed my hair and pushed it into her drooling mouth. I fumbled around, trying to loosen myself from the tangle.

Jason stood up and said, "You have never formally introduced me to your baby." He reached out, took my goo-covered hair out of Destiny's mouth, and placed it over my shoulder. The sharp and pungent scent of men's cologne drifted my way.

"Hey, baby, what's your name?" he said to Destiny.

I felt a tingle in my knees that slowly crept up my legs. I didn't know how to act, not with my baby or with Jason.

"Jason," I said, sounding stupid and feigning composure

while trying to avoid a complete mind blank, "meet Destiny."

Jason reached out and pulled Destiny out of my arms.

"Will she let me hold her?" he asked as he instinctively started to bounce Destiny on his hip.

"Not usually," I said. "But she looks okay with you so far."

Jason walked away and spoke quietly in baby talk. "Hey, Destiny, you're a cutie. You're as cute as your mama. Look at your little nose." He turned and walked back toward Kate and me. "You're lucky to have such a cute little baby."

"Yeah. She's the greatest," I said. And then it began to dawn on me what I was feeling. It had been a year ago that I realized I was pregnant, and from that moment I had put away any thoughts of the opposite sex. I had worked so hard to forget about the pregnancy, I'd kind of forgotten I had a body at all, let alone what it might feel. I made a vow to myself that day never to look at another guy until I was at least twenty-five, and it had been easy, up to now, to keep that vow. Once Destiny was born, the guys looked at me as if I had a catchy disease or as if they wanted something they thought I would give easily, and I was sure I wasn't going to have a guy in my life for a long, long time.

Now I could see how that might change. When I reached for Destiny, Jason's hands got stuck under mine. For a few seconds I felt the warmth of his hands wrapped around my baby.

"Goodnight, baby girl." This time I hugged Destiny tightly and squeezed her cheeks against my own. "Thanks, Kate," I said as Kate took Destiny out of the room and Dawna walked in.

Saved. Perfect timing, coach.

"Okay, guys, your stage manager is here," Dawna said as she placed herself between us. "Where are we? What are we doing?"

"We're putting Destiny to bed," Jason said.

"Well, that's a good thing. Get the baby to bed before we start. That's Hollywood, for sure. All the big stars bring their babies to the set—they breast-feed the kids between scenes. Everything waits for Hollywood babies. Pretty cool, eh? So we're off to a good start."

"Jane was just going to sing this song once through so I could get the hang of the tune." Jason laughed. "Not like it's going to help any."

"You want me to sing for you?" I asked.

"Yeah. Good idea. Come on, Jane. It's not like we haven't heard you sing it a million times," Dawna piped in. "Jane sings in the bath, in bed, at breakfast, you name it," she added to Jason.

Thanks, Dawna.

"No music, no props, just sing?" I said, feeling put on the spot.

"Just sing," Dawna commanded.

"Okay," I said, sort of relieved she had taken control. I took a throaty breath, stood straight, and waited a second to feel some calm. I breathed in again, but the knot in my stomach prevented the air from sinking any deeper than my tonsils. I started singing, breath or no breath.

I started the first few words. A thin, watery sound I didn't recognize emerged from my lips. The next two phrases and I was already out of breath. My voice cracked. I took another breath. The air flowed through my body down to my toes and my heels. I felt planted on the worn, brown shag carpet and spread out as the words poured out of my belly.

Jason and Dawna faded into the back of my mind as I sang.

"Wow," Jason exclaimed when I finished. "What do you need me for?"

I flopped on the old chair opposite to him. "It's a duet—I need you to sing the male part."

"Wow." Jason didn't seem to hear a word I said. "I can't believe you're so good."

"I'll help you with your part, Jason. We'll just follow Jane." Dawna stood up and grabbed one of my hands and one of Jason's. "Let's get started."

I handed Jason a song sheet. "Your part is highlighted in yellow."

I could tell that the closest thing Jason had ever gotten to singing was chanting plays in rugby, so singing a cappella with two girls wasn't going to come easily. And Jason was right—he didn't know how to sing. At first his voice was so tight it sounded like it was eking through the stretched neck of a balloon. But after we went through the song a couple of times he loosened up and didn't sound too bad at all. With some more practices I figured he might even sound good.

We sang the song a few times together and then I added dance steps.

"Left, one, two, and then two behind. Right, one, two, and then two behind," I instructed. "Good—one, two, and then back, one, two." Jason moved like the Tin Man in *The Wizard of Oz*, attached by hinges at his joints and rusty.

"Come on, loosen up," I coaxed. I reached out, and the second my palms touched his shoulders it felt as if I had hit a live wire, a lawn mower with a short, an unprotected wall socket.

Jason moved away, thankfully, and strutted around the room. "If you weren't so good, I'd sound better. But hey, I'm not that bad. Maybe I should try out for Danny Zuko."

"You've got the body—um, the moves for it." I couldn't believe what I said. "I mean, sure, you could do it. You're great. Your singing is getting really good."

"You guys are good together," Dawna said. "Really good.

Go for it, Jason. You can audition together."

Jason dropped on the sofa next to me and said, "Thanks. I had a great time tonight. I'm glad you talked me into this."

"Me too. Want to do it again?"

"Sure, when?"

Dawna got the calendar and arranged three more practices before auditions. "By then," she said, "no one will be able to beat you two."

Jason sat quietly. I watched him fidget with the hem of his shirt. "You know, Jane, I really hope you get this part. You're going to blow them away at the audition."

"I want the part," I responded. "But I can live without it. I just don't think I would be happy if I didn't try."

"Ever hear from Trevor?" Jason changed the subject.

"He promised to keep in touch, but I haven't heard from him. Have you?"

"Nobody has. We think his father told him he wasn't allowed to call anybody. His father was so pissed off with him about the baby. He wouldn't let Trevor even mention it." Jason's voice was kind. "Is it hard for you?"

"Not really. Things sure have changed. Nothing's the same anymore. But I just do what I have to do."

"God, you're strong."

"I'm a teenager too. I'd be lying if I said I didn't really wish I could be free."

I swallowed, to choke back the possibility of bawling. I didn't expect a sensitive conversation about my feelings. Only Dawna and Nurse Cindy had ever asked me how I felt. But singing and dancing and touching Jason were enough for one night—I didn't need crying as well.

I couldn't wait to see my cousins. Other than the guys who hung out with the boys, I didn't see our relatives very much anymore. Most of the kids went to the school on the reserve.

It had been six years since we lived there with Teh. The old house stood three storeys high and sat on a hill surrounded by dingy houses dwarfed by comparison. Someone had towed the house in, and instead of digging a basement, they set it up on a tall foundation. Then they never finished it off. The first floor was hard-packed dirt and rough posts and support beams for the rest of the house. No one could live down there, so that's where the other kids and I played.

I was proud of that house. It looked so grand, bright with flaked and peeled yellow paint and red trim, towering over all the other houses. Everyone on the reserve called it Teh's Big House. I loved living on the reserve. Uncles and aunties and cousins came and went from house to house. I remembered playing endlessly in the wild grass and apple trees that separated one house from the other. When it rained or snowed we ran under the house, where we dug marble pits and built forts and hideouts.

Teh's long oak kitchen table sat next to the front window. It was always set with a hot teapot, bowl of fried bread, tub of butter, jar of homemade blackberry jam, coffee whitener, and large pot of sugar neatly placed on a woven cedar mat.

Mom was born and raised in the old house along with her three sisters and two brothers. Dad moved in with her once Pete was born, and they got married. Mom stayed a Williams and named us all after her family, but it didn't make any difference. Mom and Dad knew it was only a matter of time before our family would have to move off the reserve because Dad was a white man.

Mom told me that by the time I was born it was getting

pretty bad. I remembered one night, it had been raining hard for weeks. I was listening to a steady stream of water pouring from the gutter like a waterfall. I concentrated on the water sound and hoped it would drown out the voices that were coming from the living room.

"You aren't from here, Allin," I heard someone shout at Dad. "Why the hell don't you go back to where you came from? The reserve is our land. We don't need white men living here."

"I'm from here," Mom shouted back. "And my kids are from here."

"You don't tell my son-in-law where he belongs," Teh hollered. "He's my family. Now take your cards and go home."

"Reserve's getting full of fucking white guys. I'm fucking tired of it," the guy shouted. I couldn't tell who it was, but he slammed the door when he left.

I knew the Indian reserve wasn't a good place to live for a white man. I didn't always feel like I belonged either. When my cousin Sarah got really mad at me she called me a half-breed or whitey. But life wasn't any better, as far as I could tell, now that we lived in a subdivision. It was just different. Now it was white people on Terrace Avenue who didn't want Indians living in their neighbourhood. The cul-de-sac never really felt like home. But it was where we lived and I knew we weren't going to be moving anywhere. The worst thing about the subdivision was that no one ever came to visit. Since Mom died and Teh came to live with us, she had gotten pretty lonely.

So I wasn't the only one who was excited when Boxing Day came and the family started to arrive.

"Jane, cousin! Long time no see!" Amy said as she threw her arms around me. Then Richard and Lionel and Reuben hugged me and said, "Where's Destiny? We can't wait to see her."

"Baby Jane, we haven't seen you for so long." Auntie Mabel and Uncle George stood back and eyed me up and down. "Girl, you are a beauty. We Williams sure got something to be proud of."

Soon there were twenty-five or thirty people squished together on the sofas, on the stairs, on the floor, and on benches Teh got the boys to bring up from the basement. Everyone poked and stroked Destiny. One cousin packed her for a few minutes and then another begged to hold her.

"Your baby's as pretty as you," Albert said.

"Yeah, man. Another hot Williams is on the way." Reuben laughed.

"Shut up, Reuben." I felt good. It was light. It was normal. I felt like a cousin.

When all the dirty plates and cups were stacked in the kitchen, everyone gathered in the living room. Teh pulled two chairs into the middle of the group. Auntie Mary settled on one. She pulled her heavy long skirt neatly in pleats over her knees and placed one ankle on top of the other. Her nylon stockings were rolled evenly over her black leather shoes. She rested her hands on her lap after pulling her red plaid shawl edged in silk fringe over her shoulders. Auntie Mary's face had lines on lines and wrinkles on wrinkles, intersecting like a road map of country lanes. The creases were reminders of the pain and struggle of her life, lightened by the upward turn around her eyes and mouth that made you think she laughed a lot, sometimes until she cried.

Uncle George, her son, sat on the other chair. He barely fit. The buttons on his shirt pulled at the buttonholes. Once Auntie Mary and Uncle George took their places in the centre, the family quieted down and Auntie motioned to Uncle George to speak. It's a tradition in our family for the elder to tell someone else what to say for them. It's always a man who is chosen to be the speaker.

"Mom has called us together today because she wants to give her name to the new baby." Uncle George motioned to me and wagged his finger. Quickly I realized he wanted me to take Destiny to Auntie Mary.

I placed her in Auntie's arms and then sat down. Auntie hummed almost silently as she swayed gently from side to side and stroked her twisted, wrinkled fingers over Destiny's head.

"Mom wants everyone to know that she is giving her Indian name, Say woo see wa, to this baby. In honour of my late cousin Mae, and because Mom says this baby's mother, Jane here, shows the strength, honour, respect, and dignity of the old women."

Auntie Mary tugged on his shirt. Uncle George bent down and listened while she whispered in his ear. He nodded and then spoke.

"Mom wants it to be known that this name is to be respected. That this baby is to be honoured." He paused. Auntie Mary tugged again. "Mom says she has watched Jane since she was a little girl. And especially since her mom died. Mom says Jane has the strength of the great women. She will raise this baby like the Say woo see was that have gone before."

He bent down again to listen to Auntie Mary's words. Auntie Mary knew exactly what she wanted to say, but she said it only one bit at a time. "Say woo see wa raised up her children, Mom, her brothers and sisters, by herself. She always put food on the table. She encouraged them to go to school. She taught them to respect the old ways and how to live in the new ways. This is what Mom wants for this baby girl."

Again she spoke in his ear. Uncle George turned and faced me. "This is a big responsibility for you. You are still young. But you will bring up your daughter to be a strong woman."

It was quiet in the room except for Uncle George. Everyone watched Auntie and Destiny. Destiny was wide awake but lay perfectly still, as if transfixed by an ancient silent song.

Auntie Mary tugged again on George's shirt and whispered.

"One last thing. Mom wants me to tell Jane that she is proud of her. She is proud that Jane is still going to school. Mom wants her to continue to go to school and not quit. She says education is an important thing. She knows how hard it is for Jane, but she must be strong."

Auntie Mary tugged again.

"Another one more last thing." Uncle George chuckled a belly laugh until I worried the buttons would pop off his shirt. Auntie Mary had a way of never finishing. When she had someone to talk for her and an audience to listen, she found a way to make sure her speech went on and on. Uncle George wiped his hand across his face as if to erase his smile. Then he nodded with a serious frown on his face, trying hard not to break into laughter again. "Mom says she knows Jane dreams of being an actress. She says that Jane should follow her dream. Mom wants all you young people to have a dream and to follow your dreams and to be the best you can be. She says it'll be hard for Jane to be a mother at such a young age." Uncle turned and looked at me and pointed his finger. "But she says she wants you to follow your dreams."

Auntie Mary sat quietly for a few moments until everyone began to fidget. Then she raised her hand and cast a stern, disapproving look around the room. This time she spoke loudly to Uncle George to make sure that everyone heard.

"Tell them I am sorry for such short notice. Tell Allin I want him to be part of the naming of his granddaughter. Just because Mae's gone doesn't mean he isn't part of this family."

Uncle George nodded to acknowledge his mother. He turned to face Dad, who had perked up when he heard his name, and then repeated Auntie Mary's words. Uncle George sat down, Auntie Mary turned her eyes to Destiny, and everyone watched Dad. Being a man of not very many words and used to having Mom take care of all the official family business, he gave only a short reply, and it was quiet.

"Thank you, Auntie Mary. I'll be there and do what I can. And thank you for honouring my granddaughter. It means a lot to my family."

After a little shuffle, Teh and Auntie Phyllis served tea and coffee and chocolate cookies, and the group sat back down to make the arrangements for the ceremony. Teh, Auntie Mary, Uncle George, and the other adults decided who would cook, clean the bighouse, be the speaker, the singers, who would park the cars, rent the chairs, buy the special blankets, and so on.

Uncle George led the discussion, but Teh and the women made most of the decisions. Auntie Phyllis wrote the details in a book. When she closed the covers and placed her pen on top she said, "There. We've got everything."

The meeting was over. Everyone stood up to leave.

Destiny had fallen asleep in Auntie's arms.

"Thank you. Thank you so much," I said as I leaned down to give Auntie a hug. "I will be the best mother I can be for my baby. I will raise her to be the kind of woman you are, and Teh and your mother and grandmother."

Auntie Mary ran her fingers through my hair.

"You will do fine, my girl. You will do fine." Her voice was tired and crackly. She squeezed my hands with her bent fingers. I looked at her nails. They were long and perfectly filed, each nail painted a slightly different shade of pink.

One by one the family filed out.

"See you later," I called out to the last cousin as the front door shut.

After the cleanup was done I was exhausted. Before I took myself and Destiny to bed for a nap I hugged Teh and thanked her.

She held my hand. There was excitement in her voice when she said, "We have a lot to do. It's going to be a good naming."

All the old people had Indian names and some of the young people did as well. I got my Indian name before Mom died. She knew she only had a few months left so we had a small family ceremony and she gave me her name, Tea sa. It's an old family name too, but it's not as important as Say woo see wa, not as strong.

I lay next to Destiny in bed, looking at her tiny body. She was too small to be Say woo see wa. I tossed and turned, drifting in and out of sleep.

Lemon lime green evening light, so bright it is squinty. I stand in a meadow with wild grass and buttercups next to a huge driftwood cedar chair, a throne, built with no hammer or saw, just pieces fitted together and covered by the green and red and yellow Hudson's Bay Company trade blanket that was draped over Destiny's shoulders as she sat in the chair. Tiny Destiny. But older than me. Older than old. Lifetimes old.

I drag a cedar chest, beautifully painted with a black-and-red raven swallowing the sun. The chest is heavy. I struggle alone, pulling the box inch by inch toward my daughter. Once it is at her feet I lift the lid. An enormous brass badge lies inside with a clip. Inscribed on it is Say woo see wa in a language I can't read. I hear the cedar call out the name.

I lift the badge and pin it on Destiny's blanket, which has wrapped itself around her.

I woke up and checked the time—9 p.m. I picked up the phone.

"Hey, Jane, what have you been doing?" Dawna said.

I said, "Family Boxing Day. What about you?"

"Me too, and I'm really glad everyone's gone home. Ever wonder how you got to be part of your family?" she asked. "Ever wonder if you got mixed up at birth?"

My mind went into instant replay. I thought of all my cousins and aunties and uncles. Pete and Joey, Teh and Dad. I thought of Mom and Destiny.

"No. Never," I said. "No mistakes here. I'm a mixture of my mom and dad, my cousins, aunties and uncles and grandmas and grandpas. And all the old people that are dead now."

"Really? I feel like an alien," Dawna said. I had never heard her voice sound so sad. "I'm not like my mom or my dad. Tracy and Gina, my older sisters, moved out long ago. Now they come home with their boyfriends, eat dinner, and leave. I don't fit in at all. There's my grandpa. He and my dad just glare at each other. And my grandma examines everything Mom does. Even the littlest thing, like how she dries the cutlery. It's never good enough. Half the time I go to my bedroom and no one even misses me."

"Not me. And especially not tonight," I responded. "I know where I come from, but sometimes I don't know where I fit. Sometimes I feel like a sister, but sometimes I feel like the boys' mother. Dad barely talks. Teh looks after us, but it's me that has to keep the boys in line. And now with Destiny. Talk about confusing."

"Yeah, I never thought of that part. What about her?"

"I'm going to make sure that she feels like part of a family. She is going to get her great-great-auntie's Indian name in March."

"What do you mean by that?" Dawna asked.

I explained it all. I told her how Auntie Mary was going to give Destiny the ancient family name, the most honoured of all the names for women. I told her about my naming ceremony when I was eleven, how I received Mom's name before she died—how I stood in the middle of the bighouse, draped in a silk fringed blanket while women drummed and sang and my cousins danced.

"I want you to come to Destiny's naming ceremony, Dawna. Then you'll see the whole thing for yourself," I said.

"For sure I will be there," Dawna said.

13

"Auditions are next Wednesday and Thursday after school. The first one is at 3:15 sharp. Check the schedule. It's posted on the notice board. Each audition will be given five minutes. In that time we want you to introduce yourself and explain briefly why you picked the role and why you picked the piece you're going to perform."

You could feel the tension in the crowded drama room when Mr. Knight paused. We were all hoping he would give us a clue or a jump that would help us get a part.

"I'm going to give you a little sketch of what we'll be expecting so you know how to prepare." He mocked an audition. It was pretty stupid, but we got the idea and everyone relaxed.

"We have picked a skeleton lighting and sound crew to work the equipment for the auditions. If I call your name and you *can't* make it Wednesday or Thursday, then let me know."

Dawna fidgeted side to side in her chair. For the first time I realized all the attention had been on me and the competition for my part.

When Mr. Knight said, "On the lights I want Dawna

Morgan, and Lucas Freeson as assistant," I wanted to say, I'm sorry, Dawna, for ignoring you, but instead I said, "Wow, way to go, girl."

"I got it!" she exclaimed, loudly enough for Mr. Knight and the rest of the crowd to hear.

"Yeah, Dawna," a few voices squeaked out in the crowd.

She slunk down in her chair quietly. Dawna wasn't in the habit of calling attention to herself.

"The rest of you—you can change your mind about what part you want, but you must audition the part you signed up for. We want what you've practised—we don't want any last-minute presentations. If you need to switch your audition time, let me know and we'll try to fit it in, but make sure you have a good reason."

Mr. Knight gathered his papers and continued, "If you have any questions, ask them now. Otherwise, good luck and practise hard. You have one week. See you next Wednesday."

When he had finished speaking, everyone rushed out the door to check the schedule. Dawna and I waited at the edge of the crowd while heads bobbed up and down and side to side.

Vanessa stood at the front, blocking the sheet from anyone else's view until she had finished examining the audition order. Then she pushed her way through the crowd.

"I'm on Wednesday and you're not till Thursday night. Which sucks for you. I wouldn't want to audition after my performance of Sandy," she said as she passed.

"Thanks a lot," I said as she disappeared down the hall. There was something about pushing your way to the front of the crowd and jostling a place in front of the audition lists . . . and I missed out on it.

"Well, I guess we can look at what time you're on. She didn't tell us that yet," Dawna said.

Thursday, 7:15 p.m. She was right—that was bad for me. I was the second-to-last audition. I glanced at the Wednesday sheet and saw Vanessa's audition was 4:00 p.m.

"Four o'clock Wednesday is a lot better time slot than the one you got," Dawna said.

"By the time I get up there the judges will be tired and fed up with watching," I said.

"But there's another way of looking at it too," Dawna said. She never let a thing be finished until she had looked at all sides and found at least one good thing. "You'll be one of the last ones they see. You'll be fresh on their minds. Maybe you got the best time slot after all."

"Maybe," I said. I wasn't ready to think about strategy. Just the idea of winning the part from Vanessa still seemed out of the question no matter what time I auditioned. I looked at the list again to see when Jason auditioned. "Six on Wednesday. That's good for Jason," said Dawna, looking in the same place. "He'll get to be in front of the judges both days."

The parking lot lights cast a dark blue glow over the empty spaces as we left the school to walk home. We pulled our hats over our heads, tied up our hoods, and headed up the path. It had rained constantly for the past couple of weeks and the gravel path was a series of puddles and potholes.

"You did great, Dawna," I said. "I'm sorry I didn't pay any attention to what you were doing. All the attention was on me getting my part."

"Don't worry about it. But I'm pretty happy I got it. And did you hear? Lucas is my assistant. He's not going to be too pleased about that. He's been thinking the whole time that he's number one because he's a guy." Dawna chuckled.

"And equipment is a guy thing, right?" I asked.

"That's what he says," she replied. "I told him that the

equipment doesn't know whether he's a guy or not, but he doesn't get it."

We picked up our pace. Darkness and fog were settling on the fields and we could barely see the path.

"I've talked to Mr. Knight—we might be switching our time slots," Vanessa said when I met her the next day coming down the hall. She lifted her chin with her I'm-in-charge look. "I'm not sure I can make it Wednesday."

Really. My spine uncoiled from the bottom up. Straight. I looked her—almost eye to eye.

"Yeah, of course you can't make it Wednesday. Thursday's the best time."

Her blue eyes looked like icicles, dripping cold.

"What are you saying?" she hissed.

"I'm saying you'd better have a pretty good reason because I'm going to talk to Mr. Knight as well and thank him. I'm going to give them something they won't have any time to forget." I smiled and turned my back on her.

"You better not be accusing me of cheating!" she snapped as I walked away.

"Okay, Jason," I said as he and Dawna joined me in the family room for our last practice. "Today we make good, great. We're going to knock them out."

"I'm ready," he said. "And thanks for this opportunity. I get to impress them on Wednesday and then again on Thursday."

"Okay, it's loosen-up day," said Dawna. "You guys have been good, but it still looks like you're just learning the parts."

That night it all came easy, the singing and dancing. Jason

and I flowed in and out of our parts like we were joined together. I had no stops and starts, no thinking about myself and whether I was good enough.

"Wow," Dawna said when we finally finished and flopped on the sofa. "Today you guys were *awesome*."

It hit us all. We were good. Really good.

Jason jumped up, punched the air, then grabbed me and threw me onto the floor.

"Jane, you were great," he said. "And so was I."

He began tickling me under the chin. Alarmed, I turned cold and stiff. The carpet burned my elbows. I was smothered, panicked. I pushed him hard.

"Hey, hey." He rolled off onto the floor and then jumped up. "I'm sorry. Really." He held his hand out and helped me up. "I was just playing. Are you okay?"

"Yeah," I said, my heart pounding. "I'm fine. Sorry I panicked."

We slumped next to each other on the sofa.

"Let's hear it, boss," Jason laughed, turning the attention from what had just happened. "What could you possibly tell us we did wrong today?"

"First: Don't get cocky next Thursday. You guys are great, but who knows how great everyone else is?" Dawna looked serious. "I mean it."

My heart stopped racing as Jason's body heat seeped into my pores. His arm was stretched across the back of the sofa above my head. My tightness eased up and I wanted to curl under his arm.

Don't move. Just let me lean against you. Let me feel your body. I'll just reach out my hand and rest it on your leg.

"And one more thing," Dawna continued. "You guys should look at each other. I noticed today that every time your eyes should meet you look away. What's up with that?"

I pulled my hand back, and Jason crossed his arms over his chest. An uneasy silence fell. Jason broke it. "Thanks, Dawna," he said. "I'll make sure I don't think I'm too great. It's going to be hard. How does that go?" He jumped up, posing. "*It's hard to be humble . . .*" He laughed. "But seriously, girls . . ."

"What?" Dawna asked.

"Wonder if I . . . " he stopped again.

"Wonder if you what?" Dawna said.

"Well, I was wondering if I should tell them I wouldn't mind the lead role, Danny Zuko," he said.

"Of course!" Dawna screamed. "Of course! You're great!" She threw her arms around him, kissing him on one cheek and then the other. "You would be the greatest Danny Zuko. Then you could play next to Jane."

"Are you sure? What do you think, Jane?" Jason asked.

I think I want to know how to jump up and kiss you. I want to hug you. Without freezing.

"I think it's a great idea." My hands were glued to each other so I ripped one away from the other, and as if my mind was somehow not at all connected to my body, I hit him on the shoulder.

The auditions were out of bounds to everyone except the judges—Mr. Knight, Mrs. Trenton, Mr. Henshaw, who taught English and had a background in theatre in England or somewhere, and the janitor, who belonged to an improvisation group. Other than the judges, the only ones allowed in the drama room were the sound and lighting crew.

"I wish I could tell you everything, but part of the deal

with me doing the lighting is that I'm not allowed to tell anyone what they say in there or what anyone does," Dawna said on Wednesday as she headed into the room. "It's confidential."

"Yeah, I know," I replied. "I won't even ask, I promise."

On my way home I checked my watch. 4:15. My fate was partially etched in stone. Vanessa had done her thing, and the rest was up to me.

Dawna phoned at 8:30 p.m., out of breath. "I can't tell you anything," she said.

"Thanks for that, friend," I said. "Why did you call?"

"I just had to tell you it was the most amazing thing," she said. "I made them look good this afternoon. I think even Lucas was glad I was behind the controls."

"Good for you," I said. I wanted to ask, What about Vanessa? But I didn't.

"And Mr. Knight said we were great."

"Awesome, Dawna." I couldn't imagine getting excited about operating equipment, but it felt good to hear Dawna so happy.

"I know you want to hear how Vanessa did," she laughed. "I wish I could tell you, but it's not professional. You know. But the judges are great—you don't have to worry about them."

"Thanks for that, friend," I said again.

"You're going to do fine. Trust me," she said before she hung up.

As soon as I put the telephone down it rang again.

"Hi, Jane."

"Hi."

It was quiet for a moment. It was a boy but I couldn't recognize his voice.

"It's Jason."

"Oh, hey, how did it go this afternoon?"

"I don't know," he said. "Dawna's right. Don't be too cocky—it's a whole different thing when you're up there and you know there are four judges staring at you even though you can barely see them."

"Were you nervous?"

"No kidding. I'm glad I have another chance in front of them. I'm surprised they let us do it together, now that I think about it."

"Really?" I hesitated and then asked him, "What about Vanessa? Did you hear?"

"She auditioned with Mark and then Mark had to do his separately almost right after. He wasn't too pleased with that. Pretty tense."

"Did you hear? How did they do?"

"She came out of there like she owned the place. She told Mark that no matter how it went she was going to get the part. I got a look at her today that I really didn't like."

The phone was silent other than the sound of his breath.

"I guess I better go," he said finally. "I just wanted to let you know how it went."

"Thanks a lot. I'm pretty nervous about it myself."

"You'll do great. You really will. I'll be better tomorrow too. I hope."

"Thanks, Jason. See you later."

"Goodnight."

Destiny was already sleeping when I lay down. I turned out the light and stared up at the ceiling. It was pitch-black. I couldn't get the sound of "goodnight" out of my mind. Thinking of his soft voice gave me shivers up my back and down my legs. The other words that got mixed up with Jason's "goodnight" were Dawna's "You're going to do fine."

I looked at my watch. 7:05. Why did I have to get there so early? There was no one in the hall or anywhere around. I checked the list to make sure I had the time right and circled the foyer. Wind-driven rain blasted the front doors of the school. I checked again. 7:09. Where was Jason?

I felt lumpy inside and out, like I had eaten corn on the cob or steak without chewing or digesting. I felt the familiar knot in my stomach tighten.

Come on, Jason.

I watched lights move through the parking lot and then back onto the road. 7:11.

Four minutes.

A girl walked through the drama room doors.

"You next?" she said.

"Yeah, how was it?"

"I'm glad it's over. I don't think I did so hot." Tears welled up in her eyes.

"What part did you go for?"

"Frenchy," she said. "I like that part so much. But I really don't think I'll get it. What part are you going for?"

"Sandy."

"Wow, good for you. You must have guts." Her face brightened up. "Oh, I heard about you. You must be the girl with the baby."

"Yeah."

"I hope you get the part," she said. "Good luck."

"Thanks, I'll need it."

As she turned to walk away, Jason came flying around the corner. His hair was soaked and water dripped off his forehead.

"So sorry, Jane," he said. "I meant to get here early so we had time to prepare. But my dad didn't get home until late."

He stopped and took a deep breath.

"I'm so glad you're here. I feel better already."

He had just enough time to shake himself off before we heard "Next" coming from the drama room.

"That must be us," I said and I looked him right in his eyes. This was it. Something inside was taking charge. Instead of the tension building, I felt it dropping away.

He seemed to feel the same way. "We'll do great, Jane, I know it."

"Next," someone called again.

I ran in the door, dropped my bag on the floor, and grabbed Jason's hand. I led him up the stairs onto the stage.

"That's us," I said. I positioned myself in the centre of the stage. Jason stood slightly behind.

"Name and introduction," a voice said. I couldn't see the judges in the darkness on the other side of the bright lights.

"Hi, I'm Jane Williams and this is Jason Garvey." I squinted to try and see the judges' faces, but it felt like Jason and I were the only ones in the room. "I'm trying out for the part of Sandy because I've dreamed since I was a little girl that I would be on the stage one day. I've dreamed of singing and dancing for as long as I've been able to walk and talk. And I'm trying out for the lead role because my mother told me before she died that I should go for it and be all I could be . . . so here I am."

My knees and ankles and shoulders and heart were tight and calm at the same time. My jaw was loose and my voice was strong as if it were coming through the radio. I wasn't in control. Something from outside, something I couldn't name or put my finger on, was in charge. I was the flow-through.

All I had to do was let it happen.

"Thanks a lot for letting me audition for you today," I continued.

I nodded to the judges.

"I'm ready."

Just as the music cut through the air I interrupted. "Oh, one more thing." I heard the sound people scramble around to shut off the music.

"Sorry, I forgot," I said. "Thanks to Jason, too, for helping me out tonight. He's been a really good sport. Now I'm ready."

Music. Lights. Move.

When the music stopped, sweat streamed off my cheeks and onto the stage floor. My clothes were drenched.

"Thank you." I bowed and Jason followed.

"Thanks," he said.

"Thanks a lot, you two," one of the judges said. I could see a faint outline of his face.

"That was a wonderful audition," another judge said, this time a woman. "It was a real treat for us."

"It was our pleasure." I grabbed Jason's hand again and led him off the stage. We hurried out the door. Once we were in the hall, Jason picked me up.

"Jane, you were great. We were great. That was great." He giggled.

"Thank you, thank you." I hugged him, my sweaty body against his. I was still loose, I didn't stiffen. I reached up and kissed his cheek. "Thanks a lot."

When he put me down, Joey was honking outside. I grabbed my stuff.

"I have to go," I said. "I'll see you tomorrow. The big day."

"We're supposed to know by lunchtime, so I'll see you then."

"The list isn't posted yet," Dawna said when I met her at the notice board after the lunch bell rang.

"Isn't it supposed to be here at lunch?" I asked.

"That's what they said."

Vanessa strode toward us.

"Where's the list?" she said.

Dozens of kids began to gather around the drama room door.

"You should know what's going on, Dawna. You were there, weren't you?" Vanessa asked. "What's the holdup?"

"How should I know?" Dawna said. "I only do the lighting."

"Well, what did they say?" Vanessa asked loudly. "Did they say they would have it done?"

"I don't know any more than you do," Dawna said.

I didn't believe her. Dawna was uneasy. I could tell that she knew something she wasn't telling. Vanessa knew it too.

"Where's the notice? And where are the judges?" Vanessa was getting agitated. "I looked for Mr. Knight and he's not around."

Before anyone answered she stormed off down the hall.

"I have to get back to the daycare," I said.

"I'll wait," Dawna said. "I want to be here when they post it."

I hurried through the parking lot and rain and wind. I bundled Destiny up and ran back to the school. Dawna was still waiting, but there was still no notice and no one could find the judges.

Soon Vanessa returned and announced, "I've found out where they are. The judges haven't decided yet so they went out for lunch. They aren't even on school property and the list won't be posted until after school." She looked like a lit fuse. The bomb was ready to go off any minute.

"Something's up and I bet you know what it is," she said to Dawna.

Dawna hunched and said to me, "Let's go. I'll come over to the daycare with you."

"What's up?" I said, sheltering Destiny from the wind and rain. "You know, don't you, Dawna?"

"I know what went on last night as I was packing up the equipment, but I don't know what they're doing today," she said. "I'm not supposed to say anything, but it's pretty crazy, what they're doing."

"Don't tell me exactly what they said, just tell me what's up. I won't say anything. I promise," I pleaded.

"I know you won't, but I don't like to talk when I'm not supposed to." Dawna paused. She thought for a while and then said, "It's about you and Vanessa, which you might have guessed. But you have to promise you won't say or do anything about what I'm about to tell you."

"What, what?"

"Promise?"

"Yeah, of course I promise. I'd never get you in any trouble."

"One of the judges doesn't want to give the part to you because you've had a baby. He said it sets a bad example for the other kids. Like giving you a reward. I don't think he can sway the whole vote, but he's making a big deal about it. One of the other judges is kind of siding with him. The other two judges are really mad about it. You should have heard them last night after you left. It got pretty wild."

"Damn them," I sighed. "Can't I just be a girl? Not the girl with a baby? Did they say anything about my audition?

Did they like it?" Why be surprised? What did I expect? But for a short time during all the excitement around the audition I didn't feel like *just* the girl with a baby. I felt normal, almost.

"You were awesome. That's their problem. You were way better than Vanessa. Technically Vanessa was really good, but she didn't have any pizzazz. She was stiff. They all agreed you were better. But this can't come out—unless they screw up. That's why I want to be there when they post the list."

The list still wasn't posted after last class. But I didn't want to see it anymore. Still, I packed Destiny up and walked back into the school with Joey and Kate. Dawna was already waiting in the crowd.

"Mr. Knight said he's coming in a minute with the list." She paced back and forth. "I don't know what his problem is."

Finally Mr. Knight came around the corner, walked through the crowd to the notice board, and carefully taped the top and bottom of the list to the board.

"Just move back," he said in an irritated voice. "You can see when I'm finished."

I didn't like the mood he was in. I thought he would have been one of my supporters. And Mrs. Trenton. It was probably the English teacher who put up the fuss and the janitor who supported him.

Mr. Knight dropped his head and walked straight through the crowd as students called out to him, "What took so long? It was supposed to be posted at lunch."

Vanessa hesitated and stayed back. I did too. Now the list was posted I really didn't want to look. I knew what it was going to say. When I looked up, Jason had pushed his way to the front and was the first one to see the list. He turned around after reading the names and shouted at the top of his lungs.

"Jane! You did it. You got the part. And I'm Kenickie."

He ran through the crowd, picked me up, and flung me around and around until my feet were flying like a propeller. When he finally put me down, black dizzy spots clouded my vision and my head spun. But I saw Vanessa stomping down the hall toward the staff room.

I did it! I got the role! The girl with a baby is the lead!

After Dawna congratulated me she said, "Read the list and look at the bottom of the page."

My name was written on the line after SANDY. Mark was DANNY ZUKO. Vanessa's name wasn't on the list at all and "VANESSA RICHARDSON AND JANE WILLIAMS ARE TO REPORT TO THE STAFF ROOM AT 3:15" was scrawled under the list of names.

"What's up with that?" I asked Dawna.

"I don't know," she said. "But you better get down there."

Dawna took Destiny and I entered the room. Vanessa was sitting at a table across from Mrs. Trenton and Mr. Knight. Her arms were wrapped so tightly around her chest that she looked like she could strangle herself. Vanessa's eyes darted from one teacher to the other, ignoring me altogether. The air in the room was so heavy you could almost see it.

"Yes?" I said. "Is there a meeting?"

"Hello, Jane," Mr. Knight said. "Come on in and sit down. Glad you could make it. We're waiting for you."

I hooked my butt on the corner of a chair at the end of the table and dropped my knapsack on the floor.

"You two read the list," Mr. Knight said, as much a statement as a question.

Vanessa narrowed her eyes and focused on Mr. Knight. She nodded. She looked like a cat waiting to pounce or a dog waiting to bite. She was on edge, off her game.

"Yes," I said. The dizzy excitement from getting the part and all the twirling around was replaced by uneasy doubt. My name was on the list next to Sandy. I saw it with my own eyes. But it was probably too good to be true.

Mr. Knight continued with a bland voice, "Jane got the part of Sandy. And we left Vanessa's name off the list altogether."

"Tell us something we don't already know," Vanessa snapped.

"We know this is hard for you, Vanessa, but just listen," Mrs. Trenton butted in.

"This isn't hard for me." Vanessa tried to steady her voice. "This is stupid. So this is what a student gets for working hard. Nothing. My dad is going to flip at this school."

"Hold on for a minute." Mr. Knight caught his breath and spoke directly to Vanessa. "We're here to make you an offer. Before you get too excited and say things you wish you hadn't, just listen to us."

The story was that the judges reached an impasse on whom to choose for the role of Sandy. They all agreed my audition was the best, but one judge was determined that I shouldn't get the role because of my baby. Mr. Knight didn't say who it was, but it was obviously Mr. Henshaw. And the janitor agreed until they read the criteria, which said the best person was to get the role—no discrimination.

Vanessa didn't move until Mr. Knight paused. Then she almost flew across the table and said, "I can sing better, dance better, act better. She's a teenage mom!" Her voice became shrill as she spat the words out. "And she's an Indian. Who ever heard of an Indian Sandy?"

Mrs. Trenton straightened her back and glared at Vanessa. "Watch yourself, Vanessa." But before she could say anymore,

Mr. Knight put his hand up as if to stop Vanessa from attacking him and then he continued.

"We have come to a conclusion and we are here to put it to you girls. We understand the role of Sandy will be demanding on Jane. With the baby and school work coming first, it might not work for you. However, we gave you the role because you deserve it and you need to have a chance. But," Mr. Knight stopped and pointed his finger at me, "if you don't keep up with practices and your school work, we will replace you with Vanessa."

For the first time since I entered the room, Vanessa turned toward me. She shot a glance at me and said, "You already know you can't put the time into the production. You should just tell them now."

I could hear Destiny fussing outside the door. Inside my head for a fleeting second I agreed with Vanessa. The naming, the practices, my homework, Destiny, sleep . . .

Just tell them. Thanks. It was an honour to be chosen. Give the role to Vanessa. It'll take the pressure off me.

Instead I sat back in my chair and said, "I will put everything I have into the production. And that will be enough."

The room was quiet, as if everyone was deciding for themselves if that would be enough.

"I will not let you down," I continued. "And I'm sure if I do, Vanessa will let you know."

"We're sorry to put you under this pressure, Jane, but we have to make sure the lead role sets the example for the rest of the cast." Mrs. Trenton spoke gently, as if she was relieved to say the words.

"You're sorry," Vanessa cried. "You're sorry for *Jane*. What about me?"

"Your audition was very good, Vanessa. You didn't put a second choice on the sign-up sheet, but we are offering you the role of Frenchy. This was a difficult decision. It goes against our own rules, but we're making an exception because you have worked so hard." Mr. Knight's words were slow and direct. You could tell they were his only hope of getting out of the meeting without a major blow-up.

Vanessa slumped onto the table and buried her face in her arms. When she raised her head she wiped her sleeve across her eyes and sniffled, "Frenchy? I'm offered Frenchy? That's it?"

"Yes," Mr. Knight said.

"Fine for now. You all know Jane will never do it. This is just ridiculous." Vanessa stood up and kicked her chair back. "I'll be Sandy in the end."

"And if Jane doesn't keep up, you two will switch roles," Mr. Knight said.

He looked from me to Vanessa as she stormed out the door and back to me again. "Agreed?"

I knew if I disagreed it wouldn't make any difference.

Later, when I told Dawna everything that went on in the meeting, she said, "They made the right choice. You can do it."

14

"Thanks for walking with me this morning," I said when I caught up to Dawna a week later. "Been here long?"

"No. Uh-uh. Or I would have come and got you," Dawna said. She unhooked my knapsack from my shoulder.

"Thanks."

"What's up with Joey? He hardly ever drives us to school anymore."

"The car broke down last night. Him and Pete had to leave it on the side of the road up by Middleton's farm. At least that's what they told Teh and Dad this morning."

The sun was warm, and when I breathed in deeply I thought I could smell the first hint of spring in the air—that fresh scent of new life beginning to wake up in the oak trees and the crocuses.

"I think the boys were drinking last night and got pulled over. Which would be a complete drag," I said. "So much for their promise to get it together. The last thing I need right now is for Joey to screw up and leave me without a ride. Or a babysitter. How am I going to get to rehearsals if I have to walk? Just what Vanessa's waiting for."

When we walked home that day I could barely drag my knapsack. It was full of textbooks and weighed a ton. To top it off, Destiny pooped halfway home and wasn't very happy about sitting in her warm mushy diaper. Then when we turned the corner onto the cul-de-sac, I was confronted by the sight of two police cars parked in our driveway.

"I can come in with you if you want," Dawna offered when she saw the police.

"No, it's okay," I said. "I'll call you as soon as I find out what they want."

"You sure?" she asked.

"Yeah, no problem," I said. I wasn't sure that there was no problem, but I knew if there was that I would have to deal with it myself.

One officer stood at the front door, the other sat in his police car, talking on the radio. When I neared the house I heard the officer rapping persistently on the door.

I grabbed a deep breath. "What's up?" I said, nonchalant, like police were always knocking at our front door.

"You live here?" the officer asked. His words were spoken with authority. He had the kind of voice that makes you feel guilty whether you've done anything or not.

"Yeah, I live here," I snapped.

"Anyone home?" he said. He pushed harder, more aggressive.

"I don't know, I'm just getting home from school." I cut my voice short with an isn't-it-kind-of-obvious attitude. Police had been at our house before and usually I didn't mind. I had gotten used to covering for the boys when they'd get home after scrapping it out at the park or singing too loud at the store or racing the Mustang down Main Street. The police usually treated me well, and I was always polite. But not this guy. I didn't like him right off and he didn't like me either.

I nudged between the house and the officer, opened the door, and stepped inside. This guy was tall, really tall, lanky and lean with sweaty blond hair. His cheeks were flushed a blotchy red and white. In spite of his size his face looked like a bird's. He had deep-set dark blue eyes that were too close together and a small sharp beaklike nose with splayed nostrils.

I pulled the stroller into the foyer and dumped my knapsack beside it. I turned around carefully, making sure I blocked the doorway and any opportunity the officer might have of looking in the house.

"What can I do for you?" My voice was flat, but polite. The question was slightly dishonest because I knew I wasn't going to do anything for the officer unless his attitude changed.

"I am looking for Joseph and Peter Williams. Are they home?" he said.

"I don't know. I told you, I just got home." My cheeks flushed and anger burned the skin on my face. I was furious at the boys and insulted by the way this officer looked at me. There was no innocent-until-proven-guilty in this man's attitude. Just because I lived at the same address as Joseph and Peter Williams, he was going to treat me like I had done whatever he thought they did.

"Can I come in and look?" He leaned toward the slit in the door.

"No, you can't," I said.

"Can you go see if they are home?"

"Yeah."

I shut the door and locked it. Destiny wiggled uncomfortably in her dirty diaper. I lifted her out of the stroller and lugged her around the house.

"You guys here?" I shouted down the stairs so the officer

could hear. Then I turned toward the hall and hollered, "You guys here?"

The house was filled with a hush, like someone was holding his breath—a sense of waiting hung heavy in the air. I ran down the front stairs and opened the door. Destiny whined and complained as I bounced and squished her diaper on my hip, trying to keep her quiet.

"Nope. No one's home."

"Are you sure? You didn't look for very long."

"There aren't many places to look. No one's home," I repeated.

The officer's eyes narrowed. His lips grew thin, tight, and purple. "I don't think you looked too hard, young lady. I'm going to wait outside in my car until they come home."

"Oh, that's a good idea. I bet they'll be coming right home when they see you parked out there," I said. His chin dropped. I shocked myself as well. I hadn't expected to be so lippy. But it was his look that got to me. Like I was dirt.

"Okay. I'll be back later. Here's my card. I guess you won't call me when your brothers get home?" He lightened up a bit.

"No, I guess I won't."

The officer got into his car and then I shut the door.

My blood was boiling as I swung around and shouted, "You guys better not be home."

I stormed up the stairs. I knew the boys were close by. I had that hide-and-go-seek feeling, like someone was going to jump out at me any second. I waited. Slowly the front closet doors unfolded. Pete stepped sheepishly into the living room.

"For God's sake, Pete. Hiding in a closet. You're a tough man," I said. "You must be feeling pretty good about yourself right now!"

Joey slunk out of the closet behind him.

"What do you guys think? You going to hide in a closet all your life and have your little sister take care of your problems?" My voice was shrill and sharp.

"Thanks, Baby Jane," they said in unison. Both boys slumped on the sofa.

"Don't 'Baby Jane' me." I felt heat creep up behind my ears. "And don't thank me either. And don't just sit there looking like a couple of losers. I'm tired of it. I have a baby to look after. I don't need two other babies around the house."

"Don't start screaming at us. You look like a nutcase. You should see yourself," Pete shouted, jumping straight to his anger strategy.

It wasn't going to work that day, not with me. "Forget it, Pete. Be as mad as you want. Call me what you want. Scream and swear, put me down any way you want. But you're never going to be madder than I am right now," I said coldly.

"Sorry, Jane," Joey said. He was always the first one to try and make peace.

"Sorry, sorry, sorry. That's not going to work either, Joey. You just try and get out of it by sucking up. Uh-uh. Not today. You know what you guys are going to do? You're going to phone this scarecrow guy." I tossed them the officer's business card. "And you're going to tell him that you're sitting here right now and he can come and pick you up."

"No fucking way I'm going to do that," Pete snarled.

"Yes way. Now. You got yourself into trouble and you better deal with it."

God, is that Mom speaking, or is that really me?

I tried to calm down, steady the screech in my voice. "And don't swear around Destiny," I added.

"Sorry," Pete said. He tightened his arms already wrapped around his chest. "But you can go to hell if you think I'm phoning that pig. He's got it in for me, just like all the rest of them."

"You got the number. Which one of you is going to be man enough to call?" I persisted.

Silence. My brain was about to explode. I shifted from foot to foot. I wanted to slap them or throw them out the door or bash their heads together until they pleaded for mercy. I wanted to take their stuff and throw it into the backyard, their stereo, CDs, clothes, skates, fishing poles, skateboards, video games, everything in a big pile and then jump all over it and smash it all into little bits.

"You guys decide." I tried to sound calm. "Who's going to phone?"

Both boys stared at the floor.

"You know what, you guys. This isn't about you." My anger shifted and I could feel power building up in my chest. Instantly my mind took a straight line. I knew where I was going. Exactly. "And this isn't about me. I said it before and I'll say it again: This is about my baby. This is about your niece. This is about Destiny."

There was no hum behind my ears or shift in my feet. I was steady. Both feet were planted firmly where I stood.

"I get looks from the neighbours like we're all a bunch of rowdy Indians. I just got the look from that officer, like I'm some kind of loser. But one thing is for sure, Joseph and Peter Williams. Your niece is not going to be raised with your reputation. She isn't going to grow up with lazy good-for-nothing burnouts hanging around getting chased by the police. She's going to grow up with dignity. Either here or somewhere else. You stay, guys. Be what you want to be. We'll leave."

Acid burned my eyes. I breathed deep to stay steady and keep from bursting into tears.

"Destiny's going to be treated as bad as the rest of us if the neighbours keep seeing police cars lined up at our door." The tears started. "I just turned fifteen. I can't do it all myself. You keep saying 'Good job, Jane, good job.' Well, what about you guys? What kind of job are you doing?" I wiped my nose across my jacket sleeve and continued, on the edge but still in control. "I mean it, Pete, Joey. What about you? Can't you guys help me? I have nowhere to go. What's going to happen to me? To my baby?"

Pete and Joey still stared at the floor. The room was quiet except for an oblivious cooing. Bubbles formed around Destiny's lips, followed by thick mounds of dribble, which oozed down her chin.

"Give me that thing." Joey grabbed the card.

"Don't do it, man. I'm telling you," Pete called out as Joey lifted the phone.

"Look at her, Pete." Joey pointed at Destiny. "Anyway, what are we going to do? Run around the fields forever, up to our balls in mud? Hide in closets? Don't you think they're going to find us one day?" Joey dialed the number.

Minutes later Constable Conrad knocked on the door. Joey and Pete staggered down the stairs to meet him. I watched from the window. The boys walked in front of the officer and then dropped into the back seat of the police car. Across the road Mrs. Anderson's curtain was hitched just far enough for her to see our front door. Down the road Mr. Underhill lingered in his carport and watched the patrol car pull up the road and out of sight. I threw them both a wave.

Yeah, it's us. We're just doing our thing over here.

"Okay, baby girl," I said when I finally sat down to change Destiny's diaper. "It's going to be different around here. Your mommy promises you that."

I cranked the stereo. Dance music. The kind Pete and Joey told me to turn down or turn off so they didn't have to hear it. I got out the cleaning bucket, rags, broom, and vacuum cleaner. I picked up clothes, wiped the door frames, swept the kitchen, dusted and polished the furniture, and vacuumed the carpets. I made fettuccine and set the table. I mashed some in a bowl for Destiny and filled a bowl for me. I left enough in the pot for Teh and Dad. They should have been home, but I enjoyed the peace.

"Let's eat. It's suppertime." I turned down the stereo until the house was quiet. The kitchen smelled like buttery sauce, Windex, and lemon polish. Just the way it should.

By 6:30 I started to worry. Dad missed supper sometimes, but it was less often than before. And if Teh wasn't here when I got home from school, she was *always* back by five o'clock. She *never* missed supper. I phoned Auntie Phyllis but no one answered. Auntie Irene hadn't heard from Teh, but she figured Uncle Kenny wasn't home either so they must have been together.

I bathed Destiny and put her to bed and then pulled out my books. At 8:15 I heard the front door close and someone shuffling up the stairs.

I ran out and helped Teh pack her bag into the living room. "Where have you been?" I said with relief.

"Where have I been? You know where I've been. Your brothers are down at the cop shop. Again. I got the call back at the house." That meant the old yellow house on the reserve. "I got Kenny to drive me straight over there. I've been sitting for hours."

"I made them turn themselves in," I said.

"I know. I talked to Constable Conrad. He's a bit of a straightass but it's a damn good thing."

I was surprised. I'd never heard Teh call anyone a straightass before, and she wasn't one to be damning either.

"Those boys got to start being responsible for themselves." Teh fell into her recliner. "I told them they don't come from trouble and they better not start it. This family doesn't get in trouble with the cops, except them. Their poor mother would cry if she saw what her boys were up to. And my great-granddaughter ain't going to be raised in this crap." Teh's language had really deteriorated by now. There was no question—she had had enough.

"It's going to change, Teh. I'm going to make sure of that," I said. "I'm going to make you some tea."

"Oh, that'll hit the spot. Who'd figure how stupid they can be anyway?" Teh said. "Turns out those damn boys were driving home last night and they saw the cop car coming over the hill behind them. They pulled over and jumped out of the car and started running. The cops stopped, took out their flashlights, and headed after them. The boys jumped the fence in front of Middleton's farm and took off through the field, pulling their sloppy feet and sorry butts through mud up the yin-yang. They had a pretty good lead and I guess the cops didn't think the boys were worth the mess. By the time Pete and Joey got to the other end of the field, the cops had decided to turn back. Of course the boys' car was parked right there on the side of the road, so the cops just had to get the papers and come over here to get them. It's not like those cops don't know the boys personally anyway."

"So that's what all the mud and guck is doing at the back door," I grumbled. I shook my head. It wasn't funny, but it sounded like all the other times the boys had gotten into trouble. Like something out of a cartoon.

"Why'd they run?" I asked. "Had they been drinking?"

"No. That's the thing. I don't think they drink and drive. But Joey hasn't paid his fine and Pete's still on probation for his disorderly thing in the summer. He's not supposed to be out after midnight. So they figured they would run. Now we all have to be down at the station trying to explain it to the cops." Teh curled her lips in disgust. "There wasn't a damn thing I could do so I got Kenny to bring me home."

"You eaten supper? I made some fettuccine."

"No thanks. Just tea's fine. Know where your father is?" Teh lay back.

"No. He's not home yet."

By the time I had set Teh's tea on the table beside her chair, she was snoring peacefully. I slowly walked back to my bedroom. I wished Teh didn't have to deal with the boys. She was getting too old. I wished Dad was home. A few things lined up clear in my mind as I sat on my bed surrounded by textbooks, notepads, and papers. Things had gotten a bit better when Destiny was first born. But if things didn't change, this family would slip back to its old mumbo-jumbo ways.

I dumped the mess of school stuff on the floor and sprawled out on my bed. "Well, baby girl," I said out loud. "It's you and me."

15

"Want to watch *Grease* with us, Teh?" I asked. Kate had given me a copy of the movie for Christmas, and I watched it whenever I could.

"How many times have you girls watched that movie?"

"How many times, Dawna?" I asked.

"Oh, maybe seven or eight," she laughed. "Or ten."

"Okay, we'll watch it one more time and then you're going to put it away," Teh said. "You have to create your own Sandy, not copy the movie. It's theatre you're doing, not Hollywood."

When the movie finished and the credits filled the screen, Teh clicked the TV off.

"Here, girls." She reached down beside her rocker and fumbled around for her purse. "I won big-time at Bingo so I've got something in here for you. Uncle Kenny picked these up from town." She handed me a small envelope. "One for you. One for Dawna." Teh smiled.

I opened the tiny envelope and pulled out a pair of tickets.

"They were hard to get. The only two left side by side. The last night is Sunday," Teh said.

I read the tickets. *Mamma Mia*. The musical. In the new theatre in town. $100. Each.

"Wow." My jaw must have dropped to my chest. Mr. Knight had encouraged us to see the production, but there are some things you don't bother to think about. Not because you don't want to but because there's no point. Where would I be able to get a hundred dollars to go to a show?

"Teh, thank you so much." I leapt out of my chair and hugged her. "I can't believe you did this. You spent so much money. Thank you, thank you, thank you!"

"What are the tickets for?" Dawna asked.

I handed her the envelope. "Dawna, we're going to the theatre and to a real production—*Mamma Mia*. The dancing is supposed to be awesome."

"Wow, Mrs. Williams. This is great. Are you sure you don't want to go with Jane?" Dawna asked.

"No," Teh laughed. "What does an old lady like me need to go to the theatre for? You girls enjoy yourselves."

"Thank you so much, Mrs. Williams. I can't believe I'm really going. I asked for tickets for Christmas but I never got them." Dawna got up and hugged Teh too.

Dawna arrived at my house about three o'clock Sunday afternoon, packing her knapsack over one shoulder and holding black heels and red canvas running shoes.

"We have four hours to get ready," she laughed when I opened the door to let her in. "That should be enough, don't you think?"

We ran upstairs, stopping to unhook the gate Dad had recently hung at the top. With Destiny crawling around, nothing was safe. Everything seemed like an accident waiting to happen, especially the stairs.

"Where's Destiny?" Dawna asked when she entered my room.

"She was right here when I ran down and answered the door." I looked in my open closet door and then between the bed and wall.

"Destiny!" I called out.

We rushed out the door and down the hall. I found her batting the open gate with her hand and leaning over the staircase.

"Destiny!" I scooped her up just as she was about to tumble down the stairs.

"Wow, it seems like only yesterday that she was barely moving," Dawna exclaimed. "How did she make it down the hall so fast?"

"Nothing stops her now. I have to watch her every minute. We have to lock the gate every time we come up the stairs."

"Sorry—that must have been me," Dawna said.

When we got back to my room we made two signs reading MAKE SURE YOU CLOSE THE GATE BEHIND YOU and taped one to each side of the gate. Dawna added "Help keep me safe, love, Destiny" underneath.

"Come on, baby girl. Mommy's going to lock you up," I said.

I shut the bedroom door behind us and stacked Destiny's toys in the corner: teddy bears, soft books, brightly coloured blocks, dolls—kids' Christmas presents, probably, from years before, washed and repaired. Destiny had more toys than she could play with and more shoes, clothes, mittens, hats than she could wear. Almost every Saturday Teh went out in the morning carrying her old canvas bag, empty. By the afternoon she was home, her bag stuffed full, being dragged along on top of a big ladybug or playhouse or tricycle. "When Destiny gets a bit bigger," Teh would say, "this will be perfect."

I liked what Teh brought home, at least most of it, but

sometimes I wished I could buy Destiny something new. There was no money for that. The child allowance I got from the government covered Destiny's diapers, formula and other food, and stuff I needed for myself like tampons and deodorant. The dollars left went to Kate for babysitting. So Destiny played with garage-sale toys and wore garage-sale clothes and so did I, mostly.

"Okay, Jane. What are we going to look like tonight? I brought everything." Dawna emptied her knapsack on the bed. There was a long slinky black dress, fishnet stockings, a red miniskirt and halter top to match, black pants with slits up to the knees—and that was just a start.

"Where did you get this stuff?" I asked as Dawna held the black dress up in front of her and looked in the mirror. "I've never seen you wear anything but jeans and shirts and sweatshirts and hiking boots."

"I have a closet full of clothes. Mom buys them for me. She hopes to make me a lady someday. When we go out as a family for dinner she makes me dress up. So I wear something once, if that, and then I file it." Dawna tossed the clothes in a pile.

"Teh used to buy me dress-up clothes too, from garage sales. But I had to put a stop to that—she was always so disappointed I didn't wear them. Now she can buy all she wants for Destiny." I sifted through the pile. They certainly weren't garage-sale clothes. They were all beautiful, expensive, designer clothes. Nothing I would be able to buy in a million years.

"Mom's a shopping freak. She has to have the best things and lots of them," Dawna said. "You should hear Dad and her fighting about it.

"But hey," she added after a short pause, "look what we've got to choose from. So who's complaining?"

I picked up a red miniskirt and held it up to my hips. "What do you think? Should we go really dressed up?"

"Whatever. You pick what you want. I don't know what I want to wear," she said.

"You decide, Destiny. Mommy's going to put on a fashion show for you, girl." I tried on every combination of clothes Dawna brought while Dawna and Destiny sat on the floor and watched.

"You sure don't look like you have a little baby." Dawna appreciated things I never picked up on. "The black dress shows off your thin arms and your great tan. And you've got cleavage, girl. Find a bra and stuff them in. That dress is a killer. Now all you need is high heels."

I pushed my feet into the black leather slip-ons. The slinky dress showed every curve and hollow on my body.

"Whoa, I've never worn anything like this before," I said. I looked older. Eighteen, nineteen, I couldn't tell. "What do you think, Destiny? Is your mommy ready to go to the theatre?"

Destiny yawned and stuck her thumb in her mouth.

"You look ... " Dawna stopped for a moment and thought. "Perky," she finally decided. "That's the dress for you tonight."

"But what about you? What are you going to wear?" I stared at myself. It was like someone else was standing in my body in front of my mirror.

"I just got a great idea," Dawna said. She jumped up and headed out the door. "I'm going to run home for a minute."

I studied myself in the mirror. I looked good. I didn't look like the girl with a baby. I looked like a woman old enough to be a mother. I pulled my hair up and bunched it on the top of my head. I would need earrings and a necklace. Something elegant.

This is me.

I thought of my clothes hanging out of the dresser drawers.

Jeans. Blue or black—take your pick. For me, "dress up" meant putting on my newest jeans, the least faded ones. Everyday wear meant old jeans with tears in the knees and under-the-bum cheeks. Then, to top them off, T-shirts and sweatshirts—gray, black, and maybe white. I really got creative a year before when I asked Pete and Joey to buy me a bright red sweatshirt for Christmas. I looked at my old running shoes placed side by side near the door. Other than a torn pair of elastic sandals they were the only shoes I had.

If styles had been different I might have stood out in a crowd. My clothes would have shouted out, "We don't have any money." But lucky for me most of the girls at O'Neil wore jeans and T-shirts.

Since I met Dawna I had accumulated a few extra sweaters and T-shirts. The pretty stuff. "It suits you," she would say. "It's girly." Dawna dressed the same as me, more or less—jeans and T-shirts. But there was a subtle difference. Her jeans came from the guys' department. She said they fit her better. She liked sports T-shirts, team logos. If she had her choice she would wear her Toronto Maple Leafs hat all the time, but her mom told her she would burn it if she caught Dawna wearing it to school.

Dawna's shoulders were square and her hips were narrow. The opposite of me. She was angular and looked stronger than most girls. If she paid more attention to her hair it would have been spiked. But Dawna didn't care that much about how she looked. She told me that until she came to O'Neil she was a jock. She had played soccer and girls' football and rugby.

Just as I was slipping out of the black dress, she burst into the room.

"Perfect!" she exclaimed. "And I've got the perfect outfit for me."

She pulled a black jacket and white shirt out of a bag.

"It's a tux. Well sort of a tux. Mom wore it to a costume party last year. She had it made for her." Dawna gestured to the black dress. "Put it back on and let's see how we look."

Dawna put on the black slinky pants, white shirt, and tux-like jacket. Then she pushed her feet into the red running shoes. I leaned against her for a twosome pose in front of the mirror. I had a momentary twinge of surprise at how good we looked together.

"You're awesome, Dawna. You should do the costumes for the production. Look at us. We make the perfect couple." I laughed.

"Wow," she said. "This is it."

We shaved, showered, manicured our nails, and put on makeup. When we were just about finished, Teh stuck her head in the bedroom and said, "You girls have to come out and model your outfits for us."

"We'll be right out."

Dawna wrapped my hair in a knot high on the back of my head, pulled a few stray hairs out, and then sprayed them firm, giving me that got-a-little-messed-up look.

"Okay, it's time for me to do your hair," I said.

"No way," she said. "It's fine."

"No, it's not," I persisted.

Finally she sat down and I gelled her hair and twisted and sprayed the ends.

"You look great," I said.

When we finally emerged from my room, leaving Destiny fast asleep on the bed, Teh, Dad, Pete, Joey, and Kate were waiting in the living room.

"Wow, Baby Jane." Dad's jaw fell loosely toward his chest. "Is that my little girl?"

"Cool, Dawna," Pete exclaimed. "That suit rocks."

"The limo is waiting," Joey said.

"This feels so weird," I said as I stepped out of the car and wobbled slightly onto the sidewalk. "I haven't been to town on my own since Destiny was born."

Dawna showed the tickets to the front usher.

"B-49E," he said as he pointed to the staircase to the right. "Just past the art gallery, up the stairs to the balcony, and then to your right, ladies."

We stood in the foyer for a few moments.

"Look at this place," I said in amazement. Plush burgundy carpets, heavy wooden banisters, coved and gilded ceilings, enormous gold-framed pictures—the theatre was beautiful.

When I saw the art gallery off to the side I said, "Come on, let's go see what's there."

Inside were papier mâché bodies contorted into impossible poses and placed in random spots around the room. A huge panel hung on chains from the ceiling in the centre. A mermaid was set against a sea-blue background. I stood close to the sculpture, looking. She was flying more than swimming. I had the sense she was coming out of something or going into something, I couldn't tell which.

People hemmed and hawed as they viewed the pieces. Each person stopped in front of the swinging centre panel, frowning or smiling. As I looked at the sculptures I wanted to fold my body and create a shape. An artist could paste the collage of my life on my skin, and people could stare and stroke their chins and wonder what sort of thing I was.

I watched the people coming and going, and listened. They had all been to the theatre before, and to an art gallery,

I could tell. Women walked with ease in their steps as if it was nothing at all to be balancing on heels higher than pop cans. They leaned back on their hips and chatted about the lead role in the production and the reviews in the newspaper. Men talked about investments and cruise ships and cell phone technology. Watching them, I felt like a visitor from a foreign country or an alien from another planet. But when I stood next to the sculptures, another part of me felt at home here. I felt like I was meant to be dressed in black and heels, to study art and watch the production so far away from the reserve and Terrace Avenue.

"Come on," Dawna said. "We better find our seats."

We left the gallery and filed through the crowd to the stairs leading to the balcony.

"I think I've figured out how to walk on these heels on flat ground," I said. "But stairs might be different."

I grabbed the handrail and wobbled up the stairs to the first balcony, keeping my eyes on my feet. The usher directed us toward the centre section, and as I lifted my head to find our seats my eyes fell on Vanessa walking toward us.

"Oh! Hi! Uh—Jane!" Vanessa sputtered. She looked as shocked to see me as I was to see her. "What are you doing here?"

The tone of her voice made me know exactly what she was thinking. Some people and places just don't go together. Vanessa would have expected to see me at a movie, but not at a theatre where the tickets cost $100. She wouldn't be surprised to bump into me at Wal-Mart, but she'd be shocked to see me at a brand-name store downtown, especially if I was buying something. Just *how* shocked was pretty obvious from how long Vanessa left her mouth open.

"Hi. I'm here to watch the show," I said.

"Huh? What?" Vanessa shut her mouth at last and reached

her arm out as if she was missing something she'd been holding onto. "Mark?" She tugged him toward her and leaned on him like a bent willow. Her eyes darted from my hair to my shoes to my arms and dress. That was the first and only moment up until then that I had ever seen Vanessa stuck for words.

"Hey, Jane! Over this way. I found our seats," Dawna said. She hurried down the steep steps and stood next to me. "We're in the centre, just two rows up. We've got some great seats."

I had caught Vanessa off guard. Now she glanced quickly at Dawna's *faux* tux and slit-up-to-the-knee black pants and instantly regained her control. She lifted her chin and shot a look at me. "So are you two a couple?" she sneered.

"Yeah, we're a couple." Dawna grabbed my arm. "And the Queen is dating Mother Teresa."

She pulled me toward our seats. I wiggled past the knees and purses, precariously balancing on my heels until we reached our seats.

"Perfect," Dawna gushed as we sat down. "This is awesome. A perfect view of the stage."

She completely ignored what had just happened. Did Dawna and I look like a *couple* couple?

Vanessa and Mark sat down two rows below us and over to the left.

"Poor Vanessa," Dawna laughed. "She's sure got some bee up her butt about you. But she's going to have a hard time watching the show if she keeps twisting her neck around to stare at you. You're too good for her tonight."

No matter how I looked or acted, there was no way in a million years that I was too good for Vanessa. She wanted me to know I wasn't good enough. People like Vanessa had a way of giving me that not-good-enough feeling, and since Destiny was born it was hard not to let it get to me.

But tonight I wasn't going to give her that.

I swallowed the feeling back down. I didn't look at Vanessa. I looked at the ceiling, carved with grapevines and chubby cupids, and the ornate mahogany posts and banisters, and the burgundy velvet curtain draped across the stage, so thick and plush I wanted to run onto the stage and wrap myself in it.

16

I closed my eyes when the lights came on at intermission and stayed for a few extra moments on the stage with the dancers.

"Come on, let's get something to eat," Dawna said. "Watching those dancers made me hungry."

I stood up and saw Vanessa standing at the balcony, so we hurried through a side exit and down the stairs.

People filled the foyer, standing shoulder to shoulder. We wound our way through the crowd until we found the concession, which sold only hard candies and chocolate bars.

"Where's the hot dogs and potato chips?" I said. My stomach was growling. In all our excitement to get to the theatre we hadn't eaten any supper.

"God," Dawna said. "She can't leave you alone."

Vanessa and Mark had moved in behind us in the concession lineup. At first Vanessa kept her back to us, whispering in Mark's ear. Then right out of nowhere she turned and said, "The part was mine. I'm the one putting all the work into the production. All you do is go to rehearsal."

Her flesh-tone silk dress blended into her milky skin, making her look faded under the bright concession lights.

How inconvenient it must be to get your tan from the tanning store—miss a few months and you turn transparent. Vanessa didn't only look pale, she looked ghastly thin. The starve-yourself kind of thin.

Red blotches crept up her neck and behind her ears.

She had caught me by surprise. Since I got the Sandy role, Vanessa had only shot angry looks my way. I had heard some things she said behind my back, like she was going to get her father to take back the money he had donated to the production if they let me keep the part. And someone said she had told Mr. Knight that I was having trouble at home and he should look into it. But so far she hadn't confronted me.

"I'm the one who got private lessons. I'm the one who organized bottle drives and bake sales. You think I like doing all that stuff? I did it for the part. And now . . . "

All of a sudden Vanessa looked like she was going to cry. I wondered for a second whether this explosive change of pace might be part of Vanessa's method for getting her own way, but maybe she wasn't as in control of things as I had always thought.

"Jane, you'd be so good as Frenchy. I can't play that role. I hate it. I'm crap at it. Please, Jane. Why don't we trade roles? There's still time. Please," Vanessa begged. She clasped her hands and bent her knees in front of me. Not being used to anyone begging from me, especially not Vanessa, I stepped back and reassessed the situation to make sure I wasn't dreaming.

"Please, Jane."

"No" was all I could say. I didn't feel sorry for her. I felt sort of disgusted and didn't know words that fit. I picked up my food and turned to walk away. Mark reached out and caught my arm.

"Jane," he half whispered. "Vanessa's really messed up about the part. You'd be great as Frenchy. Isn't that the other part you signed up for?"

I stared at him and said, "Forget it, Mark. Don't embarrass yourself."

Mark put his arm around Vanessa as she slumped against him. The whole thing was really pathetic. At that moment I wondered how I had ever felt intimidated by her, but at the same time I knew that she wasn't finished with me.

It was my luck to get Mr. Henshaw for English in the second semester. He let me know the first day that I better not ask for special treatment. "Having a baby is no excuse not to get your work done," he said. "I just want to warn you now." But it wasn't until the Wednesday after the show that I got to see how he really felt.

Once the class was settled he walked from student to student and tossed our papers on our desks. "Here are your book reviews. Read my comments carefully."

When he reached my desk he said, "I want you to see me after class."

I looked through my paper for comments, but there were none.

"Yes, Mr. Henshaw," I said once everyone had filed out. "You wanted to see me?"

"You think that's a book review?" he said.

"Yes."

"That's a personal opinion," he snarled. "I don't want your opinion. I want a review."

"I don't understand."

"Then maybe you better listen in class," he said.

"But I—"

He interrupted. "Don't 'but' me. I'm tired of you thinking you can do anything you want in this school. We don't need young girls with babies parading themselves around here as if it's something to be proud of. You think you can drag your baby to the daycare and then come to school as if you're a normal teenager. Then you do half-assed work and expect me to give you the grades so you can be the star in the show."

"I'll redo the book review," I said.

"And you'll do it right." He lowered his eyes. "I'm warning you—I was talking to Mr. Knight and told him that I'm not very happy with the work you're doing or your attitude."

When I walked out of the classroom I felt my blood drain to my feet.

Parading myself around, drag my baby, normal teenager, half-assed work, the star of the show . . .

The words repeated themselves in my head, but they made no sense. There was nothing I could do to change any of it. But he had the power to convince Mr. Knight and I knew it.

As Dawna and I headed toward the daycare for lunch, a group of tall bulky guys sauntered past us in the hall. A bronzed blue-eyed blond guy swaggered in front of the others. He slowed down and deliberately eyed me up and down.

"You're the girl with the baby, right? The girl in *Grease?*" he called out. When he got close enough he reached out and grabbed my butt. Not a little tap or even a flat-hand slap. He grabbed my butt, held on, and pinched it until it hurt.

"I hear that's just what you are—well greased. Easy to spread. Maybe you could spread those gorgeous legs for me." He said it loud enough for everyone standing around to hear.

Kids turned in shock and stared at him and then at me. I couldn't move, my blood curdled, I felt woozy and faint.

"Yeah, spread them for me too," his friend called out.

Dizzy, I slunk to the side of the hall and leaned against a locker. I turned just in time to see Dawna whirl around and bolt toward the guys.

"Shut up, you ugly piece of crap!" she shouted. "You think she'd even look at you? You loser."

I wanted to call out, *Leave it alone, it's okay,* but I was numb. When Dawna took a swing at the muscly blond guy I couldn't believe it. What was she doing?

Just then I caught a glimpse of Vanessa laughing. "Look, how cute. The dyke's defending her girlfriend," she said, loud enough so everyone could hear.

"Fuck you, asshole," Dawna screamed. "And fuck you too, Vanessa."

Everyone in the hall stopped and gawked at the ruckus.

"Get out of here, bitch. You crazy?" one guy said to Dawna as he grabbed her flailing arms and pinned them behind her back. She kicked frantically. My numbness disappeared when I saw Dawna drive her hiking boot right into Blond Jock's shins. Shocked by the pain he staggered backward. Immediately he rebounded and raised his fists.

"Come on. Let's go. Let's go," he said. He bounced back and forth like he was a boxer challenging a champion. Dawna would have given him a good fight if the other guy had let her go.

For an instant I was scared for Dawna. But then the whole thing got kind of out of control. There was the jock, head and shoulders towering over Dawna and bouncing around like an idiot, as his friend struggled for all he was worth just to pin her hands behind her back. Their friends were standing around shouting, "Get her, Ryan. Get the bitch." And then there was Vanessa laughing hysterically.

The scene looked completely stupid, but the crowd was shocked—no one knew for sure whether Ryan would throw a punch or not. Dawna wrenched violently, trying to free herself. At the same time she swung her boots wildly, grazing the legs of Ryan's supporters.

"Tell your friend to let me go or I'll kick your ass," she shouted.

Nobody expected what came next. Dawna wound up and aimed her heel directly behind her. It landed squarely on the shin of the guy who anchored her down, like a loose bolt of electricity. He tossed her across the hall and then he collapsed on the floor, grasped his shins, and moaned in agony. Dawna fell flat on her butt, bounced once on the floor, and then sprang back to action. The guys were already running down the hall. She took off after them, leaving their injured buddy grimacing on the floor.

The tense quiet that hung over the crowd was interrupted when someone blurted out, "That's one kickass girl." Then everyone erupted into laughter. Guys shouted, "Big mouth, Ryan. Why don't you learn to shut your face?" "Girl's gonna get you, Ryan." Others laughed at the one groaning on the floor and called out, "Got no balls now, hey, Mike. You guys really rock."

Unprotected by his friends, Mike scrambled to his feet and hobbled off without a word.

As the crowd disbanded, kids shouted at Dawna, "Way to go, girl." One girl walked by me and said, "They're gross. To everyone. Don't take it personally. Some of us got a lot of respect for what you're doing."

Dawna shook her legs and rolled her shoulders. She ran

her fingers through her hair as she walked back down the hall. She was furious. To say I had never seen her look like that before would be an understatement. I don't think anyone in the hall that day had ever seen anything like it.

"Fuckin' pigs," she mumbled under her breath. "Like you would give them one look," she snorted, "pieces of crap." She rolled onto the balls of her feet and slapped her thighs. "Fuckin' pigs," she repeated.

"You all right?" I asked when she joined me by the lockers. "I had no idea."

"No idea of what?" she said. Her eyes darted down the hall and side to side. Adrenaline was still pumping. I didn't know what to do. Dawna was better at comforting me than the other way around. I gingerly placed my hand on her shoulder. She stiffened as if she might explode.

"No idea of what?" she asked again.

"No idea you were so tough," I said. Then paused. "I had no idea you would stick up for me like that."

She loosened up.

"Thanks," I said. "No one has ever defended me like that before. You were great."

"They're stupid, Jane. Don't listen to them," Dawna said. "I'll get those little suckers if they ever say stuff like that again. They're full of crap. You know that, don't you?"

"Yeah, I know that," I said. "Thanks again."

I knew the guys were big, full-time losers. I knew I shouldn't listen to them. But what else can you do but listen when someone shouts at you in the hall? It was worse than I imagined—the words they said were so gross. I didn't think words could hurt so bad. Ever since I got pregnant I had worried about what people would say about me, and then Destiny got born and I thought I was getting over it. Now to hear it said, so mean, in front of everyone; unable to defend myself, and then the other kids coming to my defence . . .

"Thanks for being such a good friend," I said.

We stood quietly for awhile.

"Vanessa better quit with her crap too," Dawna said.

I swallowed hard and said, "It's not true, is it?"

"We're friends, Jane. You're the best friend I've ever had. Don't listen to what she says."

That was enough for me. I didn't care what Vanessa said about Dawna. I thought about how Dawna had pulled herself together after chasing the guys down the hall and I was proud of my friend. I rolled my shoulders back, ran my fingers through my hair, took a deep breath, and said, "Okay, let's go." I wasn't as sure as Dawna, but it was better than running and hiding and letting jerks wreck my life.

17

Sometimes eight months can go by and the world doesn't change much. Then there are eight months that seem like forever, another lifetime, and when you look up ahead you know nothing will ever be the same again. The eight months between July and March were those sorts of months. Destiny, homework, family, Dawna, the daycare, my old friends, rehearsals, rehearsals, rehearsals. Everything had changed and now life moved so much faster and required so much more from me. It was March 27, eight months since Destiny was born.

Auntie Mary had decided on this day for Destiny's naming. She said it had to do with her grandmother's birthday, but I couldn't figure out how it fit. The old women in our family liked symmetry. They liked things that repeated in an orderly way, things that tied together.

The day began slowly. I needed time to prepare myself, to steady the pace so things didn't get away on me. Ceremonial days were like sending a toboggan off the top of a long steep hill—once you pushed off there was no turning back. Not until it was all over and you were left winded.

I sat on my bed. I wanted a few more minutes alone with Destiny.

"You roly-poly pudding and pie," I said. The rhyme kept repeating itself in the back of my mind, but I couldn't get the words right. "How does that go? Roly-poly? Pudding? Oh. Oh, yeah. 'Georgie Porgy, pudding and pie, kissed the girls and made them cry.' That's it."

The words of nursery rhymes came up from memories I didn't know I had. Mom must have sung them to me and now here I was singing them to Destiny. Why do people say stuff like that to babies? It sounds so dumb when you listen to the words.

Kissed the girls and made them cry.

And then what about Rock-a-bye Baby? I sang it to Destiny all the time.

Down will come baby, cradle and all.

I hoped Destiny didn't understand the words I was saying. The trouble was I didn't know any other songs to sing to her except for rock songs, and they didn't seem appropriate either.

"Today, baby girl, you're the guest of honour. Naming day for you. We better dress you up 'cause everyone's going to be looking at you today," I said. I heard feet shuffle in the hall, dishes clink in the kitchen, and coffee being poured.

Relatives had been arriving since the previous afternoon. Teh and I made up beds in the living room and the family room downstairs. We borrowed cots from Uncle Kenny, laid out our foamies, and pulled out the sofa bed. We had enough sleeping spaces in the house for eighteen people including our family. Every bed was being used and there might have been a couple more than eighteen if you counted the kids who curled up with their parents.

I laid out Destiny's clothes on the bed—blue denim

overalls and a pink turtleneck. I took my time dressing her and putting her hair in tiny ponytails to prolong our peace and quiet for as long as possible. When I opened the door the hall was full of people waiting for the bathroom.

"Hey, cousin. Can I hold your baby?" Richard asked.

Whether Richard was my cousin or not depended on what you called a cousin. On the Indian side of my family, the side we hung out with most, we called anyone cousin who was too closely related to us to marry. That's how the old people made sure we didn't date our relatives. It seemed like everyone was related. If our parents were cousins, or if our grandparents were cousins, then we were cousins. Sometimes it got complicated, like with Richard, my cutest cousin. His mom used to be married to Mom's cousin—for a few years—so ever since we were kids we called each other cousin. His family lived on the mainland and we didn't see each other very often, but we had always secretly flirted, making sure of course that Teh didn't find out, or Mom or Dad. Since we found out we weren't blood related there had been added tension between us.

He took Destiny out of my arms. "Wow, I didn't think *you* would be the one to get pregnant," he said. "She's sure cute. Just like you."

What should I say? Thanks for thinking my kid is cute? Thanks for telling me how disappointed you are with me?

"Yeah, well, I did." I left Destiny with him to work her magic and went into the kitchen.

It was only 8 a.m., but everyone was up. The beds in the living room were rolled up and stuffed in the corner of the room. Cousins and aunts and uncles drank coffee and ate eggs, bacon, fried bread, toasted waffles, toast, cereal, and anything else Teh prepared in the kitchen. Auntie Mary was already sitting in the armchair, drinking coffee and checking on final preparations.

"Morning, Auntie," I said. "Have you had breakfast?"

"Not yet," she answered. "I'm fine here. I just need a refill on the coffee and maybe a little toast. And jam. Blackberry if you have it. And maybe a little bacon—just a few slices, and only one egg—not too well done. I can smell it cooking in there. And a bit of sugar with the coffee, and cream."

Auntie Mary had a way of knowing exactly what she wanted and how to get it. I think that's why ceremonies always went off without a hitch. It was the attention she paid to detail.

That morning the house reminded me of Teh's old house when Mom was alive. The busy hum of kids playing, old people chatting, teenagers laughing, and women in the kitchen cooking and serving. In my family it was the women who were in the kitchen because that was where things got done. Family decisions were made in the kitchen. Plans were made in the kitchen. Advice was given and received in the kitchen. And although the chiefs and councils were mostly men, reserve issues were settled first around the kitchen table.

Auntie Phyllis had arrived and was already standing at the sink, up to her elbows in dish suds. Dirty supper and breakfast dishes were piled on her left, and mounds of clean dishes were stacked to dry on her right.

"You get a cloth and dry these things," she called out as a young girl walked by and picked up some toast. "And then go out and see if anyone hasn't eaten."

When I finished getting Auntie Mary her breakfast I stood next to Teh as she dropped dollops of dough into a cast-iron fry pan bubbling with hot oil.

"Can you take over for me here, Jane?" she asked. She wiped her forehead with the corner of her apron.

"Sure," I said. I picked up two forks and lifted the corner of the sizzling bread to check if the small mounds were ready to turn. I could already feel the hot greasy steam settling on my face and arms. Nothing was better than eating fried bread, but nothing was worse than cooking it.

Teh pulled her apron over her head and wiped her face again. She straightened out her new velour pantsuit. It had taken her days to decide what to wear for the ceremony. It wasn't until the previous Saturday that she finally found the perfect outfit.

"Jane," she had called out when she got home from shopping. "I got it and it's perfect." I didn't know what she meant. "It" could have been anything.

She dug around in her bags and pulled out the pantsuit. "Twenty dollars," she said with glee. "The woman wanted thirty but I wasn't going to go anywhere near thirty dollars. I said twenty and stuck to it and finally she went for it. Look, the magenta reminds me of the gladiolas I used to grow at the old house."

Teh had loved her gladiola patch next to the front stairs at the old house. She dug the bulbs deep into the soft soil. She watered and weeded the plants and strung them to posts when their long stems grew taller than me. I remembered the day Uncle Kenny's son Donnie lost control of his dirt bike. He had been doing donuts around the circular driveway. Each time he turned in front of the stairs he spun the back wheel of his bike and dug a hole in the gravel. The bike shook when he hit the hole, which got deeper with each lap. I stood on the steps and watched as he revved the engine and circled for another turn. As he neared the hole, instead of turning, the bike hopped the hole and shot directly into Teh's gladiola patch. Luckily the soft soil slowed the bike down, and Donnie just slightly dented the side of the house and broke only a small chip off the side of his front tooth. I knew it could have been much worse, and in the end the gladiolas were a good thing. They saved a lot of damage.

Teh didn't see it that way. She stormed out the front door, yelling at Donnie and waving her hands at the bent and broken flowers. She said she would rather have Donnie lose both his front teeth and spare her flowers. That way he would have learned a lesson. Teh never replanted her garden next to the house. Since then she wore the colours of the gladiolas—orange, gold, magenta, violet . . .

I fried bread until the sticky dough was finished and then turned the stove off, picked up the coffee pot, and headed into the living room.

"Anybody?" I said. "More coffee?"

I refilled cup after cup.

"Sugar?" old Uncle Remi asked. "Got any?"

I got the bowl and shoveled three heaping teaspoons into his cup. He held it out for more.

"Uncle, you better be careful with your coffee and sugar," I said.

"Just one more, honey. Your old uncle is still a little sour this morning," he said. I heaped another spoonful into his cup. "That's a girl."

Auntie Mary's eyes followed me around the room.

"Say woo see wa," I said to her. "What does that mean?"

I hadn't talked to Auntie Mary very much. I wasn't afraid of her, but I was always extra cautious when I was around her. It felt like I was being watched, that everything I did was stored in her memory, to bring up sometime in the future. So I had a keep-my-distance feeling with her. I knew the other teenagers in the family felt the same way. When Auntie Mary cleared her throat, people would stop what they were saying and wait for her to speak. Sometimes she would clear her throat a few times and then wait until the room was completely silent before she would say anything. She liked the in-between time when everyone's eyes were focused on her.

"Spring rain," she said after a while. "Say it again for your aunt."

"Say woo see wa," I said slowly and deliberately, making sure to start and stop the syllables exactly the way I had heard the old people say the name.

"Oh, you sound like music to my old ears," she said. She squinted until the slits of her eyes were so narrow I was sure I had disappeared completely out of her sight. "You sound like the old people. They sang when they spoke, and you do too."

"Tell me, Auntie, where does the name come from?" I asked.

"What is the name?" she said. "Say the name. Keep repeating it. Let me hear it one more time."

"Say woo see wa," I said.

"That's it. My aunt carried that name and my grandmother and her mother before that. They were given the name when they had their first period and became women. They were instructed to give life to our people, just like the spring rain. My grandmother had ten children, and by the time she passed away she had forty-six grandchildren and I never did know how many great- and great-great-grandchildren."

"I don't think Destiny will have that many children."

"No, I don't think she will. But you'll teach her to take care of the people. I watch you and I know you will guide her. We need women like you, Jane, and like your mother. You have taken after her." She placed her hands on my shoulders. "This may feel like a heavy weight now. But you're young yet.

You might think that bringing up this baby is a hard job and you'll get tired and scared. But it's an honour you've been given. You raise Destiny up to be respectful. Our people will be proud of her. And you."

She dropped her chin onto her chest, which was Auntie Mary's way of letting you know she was finished speaking. After a brief pause she looked up at me sharply.

"I need more coffee. Where did you put that pot?" She reached for her cup. "And does your Teh have any more of that fried bread?"

I nodded. "And that blackberry jam too, right?"

"Oh, yes. Not just a little dab either. You make sure I can taste it, will you, honey?"

Teh stood at the top of the stairs, one hand on her hip and the other directing the activity at the door.

"Do you have the blankets from the closet in the family room?" she asked.

"Yeah, Dad took them with the first load," Pete called up the stairs. Of course Dad took the first opportunity to get out of the house so he didn't have to socialize. He would be happy once he got to the bighouse, where he could keep himself busy wiping the bleachers and sweeping the floors of the kitchen, without having to talk to people.

Since the planning meeting, family members had been bringing stacks of boxes filled with blankets, towels, dishcloths, dishes, plastic cups and glasses, candles, jewellery, kids' hats, candies, and toys. I stood at the door and watched my brothers and cousins carry the boxes to the waiting cars.

Across the street I saw Mrs. Anderson's spindly fingers tugging at her front curtain. She must have been thinking we were finally moving out. Mr. Underhill would be pleased to think that this might be the last time he would have to put up with his quiet neighbourhood being taken over by hordes of Indians.

"Not going to get anything else in the Mustang," Joey shouted to Teh. "It's full and I'm going over to the bighouse."

"Got a little more room in Uncle Kenny's wagon," Pete called. "He'll be going soon too."

Once Pete and Joey got into helping out, they were pretty good at it. They were especially cooperative that morning because all the cousins were helping as well.

Kate ran up the stairs. "They'll need to make one more trip and then all the stuff will be out of the family room," she said to Teh.

"Okay. Tell the boys to hurry back once they've unloaded. We need to get the food over to the cooks. They're waiting for it in the kitchen."

Teh and Auntie Phyllis began unloading the contents of the fridge and cupboards. I carried the food and stacked it on the stairs and in the foyer. There were plastic hampers filled to the brim with potato salad and garnished with sprigs of parsley. I carefully layered trays of chocolate cupcakes decorated with pink icing and tiny candy hearts on top of pans of deer and moose meat, baked salmon, ham, and turkey and fried chicken. I placed trays of breaded fried oysters and pots of steamed clams swimming in murky gray water next to bags of freshly baked buns and bowls of fried bread. The sight and smell of all the food reminded me I was starving, so I grabbed a baloney sandwich from under cellophane wrap and stuffed it in my mouth.

Auntie Rachel tossed the last few cherry tomatoes on the salad, covered it with foil, and handed it to me.

"Any more?" I called out to no one in particular.

For the past few days our kitchen had been a hub of

organizing, boiling, baking, peeling, tasting, commenting, and laughing. Teh, Auntie Phyllis, Auntie Rachel, and Auntie Gwen gathered early in the morning and didn't finish until they had eaten enough off each plate to call it supper.

"Any more?" Auntie Rachel repeated.

Teh eyed the pile of food that lined the stairs and blocked the front door. I watched her stroke her chin as she checked off her mental list.

"Sandy's making apple crisp and delivering it. Colleen's bringing the hot dogs for the kids. Charlotte's making the chowder down at the bighouse kitchen. And cooking the crabs. Dennis is bringing the octopus."

She paused and reviewed the pile again.

"Get one of the boys to haul up the juice from the basement. And the tea, coffee, salt, pepper, it's all here."

Auntie Rachel and Auntie Phyllis joined Teh at the top of the stairs, eyeing the heaping trays of food.

"We might need more sandwiches . . ."

After a short silence it seemed all three women were satisfied.

Teh pointed to the clutter in front of the door and said, "Just make sure there's enough room to open the door."

I shuffled the food and opened the door and was surprised to see Dawna, hand up, ready to knock.

"You got here!" I said. "Come on in and meet my family."

I ran upstairs and dragged Dawna from one uncle to the next and from cousin to cousin. "Meet Dawna," I said. "She's my best friend."

When all the food was packed, one by one everyone wedged themselves in their cars and drove off to the bighouse. The house was empty except for Teh, Dawna, Destiny, and me. We walked around checking the fridge, cupboards, shelves, and corners for anything that might have been left behind. Finally Joey returned from the last trip carrying the juice canisters, and we piled into the Mustang.

When we pulled up to the front of the bighouse there were already dozens of cars. People were filing into the kitchen while others hung around chatting on the porch.

"I guess we are the guests of honour," Joey laughed as he parked by the front door.

Inside the kitchen the cooks had set rows of tables neatly with vases of carnations. A steady line of hungry people snaked along the buffet table, filling their plates with mounds of food. After one person finished eating, another took his place at the table. The meal was orchestrated and yet there was no conductor. People came and went in perfect timing.

I wasn't hungry, but Dawna and Destiny were so we lined up at the buffet.

"Oysters," I said to Dawna when I saw her dip a spoon into the bowl of slimy mounds. "Try them, they're great."

Dawna spooned the seafood onto her plate. When we reached the table I watched her cautiously place a small corner of an oyster in her mouth. She rolled her tongue and in a reflex motion she spewed the food onto her plate.

"EEE . . . *Jane*," she squealed.

I laughed. "It's okay. I think they're gross as well."

When we entered the bighouse, a low cloud of smoke hung almost down to the packed dirt floor. My eyes stung with salty tears.

"Don't rub your eyes," I warned Dawna. "It's the worst thing you can do. If this is a good night the fire will settle down in a little while and your eyes won't hurt so bad."

Elders on the first row of the bleachers sat shoulder to shoulder. Young people, adults, children, babies filled the stands. Everyone was wrapped in winter jackets and blankets.

The fire roared through cedar logs piled like matchsticks—matchsticks as thick as telephone poles and as long as Volkswagens. Flames licked the air before they were sucked through the opening in the roof and out into the evening sky.

"This is so cool." Dawna's red and watery eyes flitted from one thing to the next.

Teh led us to folded, brightly coloured blankets set out in the middle of the bleachers. We sat in front of the fires and within minutes Destiny fell asleep in my arms.

Old men wrapped in blankets gathered in the centre of the bighouse. Uncle Will, the speaker the family had hired, spoke to one person and then the next, nodding slowly as if to show that he knew what he was supposed to say. The young men brought a chair into the centre of the group and led Auntie Mary to sit down. Uncle Will bent beside her and listened as she spoke in his ear. Teh, Auntie Phyllis, and some of the rest of the family pinned money onto the blankets of the men standing near the fires.

One by one, women, each carrying a drum in one hand and a drumstick in the other, stepped up and formed a line at the end of the bighouse. Their heads were wrapped in kerchiefs, black or red paint was wiped on their cheeks, and blankets hung like banners over one shoulder. Slowly they began to pound. I watched Destiny's tummy rise and fall to the beat of their drums.

When the ceremony began, Destiny and I were led to the centre of the bighouse to stand on blankets carefully laid between the fires. Auntie Phyllis stood behind me to guide me through the activities.

"Auntie Mary wants me to tell you that you are her granddaughter and this baby is her great-granddaughter," Uncle Will said as the crowd settled and became quiet except for the noise of the fire crackling and children shuffling in the bleachers. "In our Indian way we have no nieces and nephews or aunts or uncles. The children in our family are our sons and daughters, and the old people are our parents and grandparents. She wants you to know that, and to teach your baby the Indian way."

Auntie Mary sat in her chair and choreographed each event by pointing her ancient finger and tugging the shirts of the men to whisper in their ears. She told them the words she needed spoken, the names of people she wanted honoured and those she had chosen to witness the naming of her great-granddaughter.

I stood quietly as blankets and money were exchanged. Men stepped forward and presented long speeches in SECOTEN. I didn't understand a word of it, but I watched them pointing from one person to the next. I could tell they were recalling ancient history of our family and how we have helped other families and how they have helped us. Uncle Will called the Indian names of people around the room. Certain people were honoured while others were asked to witness the ceremony. Some spoke to me about our family history, others about how I should raise Destiny, telling me to keep to the ways of the old people and always respect and attend the ceremonies.

Dancers spun around the fires. Drums and songs and feathers and cedar boughs and water and masks and rattles and smoke swirled around us as Destiny slept peacefully in the noise and commotion. Finally Auntie Mary stood up and shuffled to a waiting space on the bleachers. Auntie Phyllis led me from the centre of the bighouse. As soon as I stepped off the blankets, young women rushed forward, grabbing for them. After a brief rumble one woman won the blankets, the floor was empty, and the ceremony was over.

I sat back down between Dawna and Dad.

Pete and Joey and some of our cousins hauled the boxes of goods into the middle of the floor. Relatives brought clothes hampers full of blankets they had collected for the celebration. Auntie Mary had brought boxes of toasters, fry pans, bread makers, and blenders from the States, and Uncle George brought crates of flour and rice and tea and coffee.

I found the box of children's books, caps, mittens, stuffed animals, and candies that I had collected.

"Come on, Dawna, help me out," I said.

Dawna carried the box while I gave all the little children a gift along with a bag of candy and an apple.

"This is better than Christmas, Jane," Dawna exclaimed.

Later I explained the ceremony to Dawna. "It's the way oral societies, ones that don't write stuff down, do things. In the old days there was no government office for registering someone's birth or name, or a death or marriage. The old people didn't write history books and teach the stories in schools. When something happened in their family they invited the community to a gathering and asked the people to act as witnesses, to hold onto the history and the knowledge. That's why the speeches are so long—each person tells the stories they've heard, so our history stays alive. This ceremony was to register Destiny's name as Say woo see wa. Now no one can use that name without contacting us and receiving permission. Now everyone at the ceremony tonight knows that we are part of that name."

It hadn't made much sense to Dawna while it was going on, but she had still sat motionless, absorbed by every movement, sound, and smell.

"Wow," she said when I finished explaining.

18

A shift took place after the ceremony. From high gear to out of control. Two mid-terms, an essay for Mr. Henshaw, and a science report. Three weeks to the first performance. Three rehearsals the next two weeks and then two dress rehearsals the final week. If I had known during auditions what I knew then I might have gladly given the lead role to Vanessa. Mr. Knight didn't only want me to perfect the role of Sandy, he said I also had to be an example to the rest of the cast. "That's what being the lead means," he said. He constantly lectured Mark and me on setting a high standard for the other performers. If I was one minute late he reminded me of what I had said. "You said you could do it, Jane. I believed you," he nagged. "Now don't let me down."

Vanessa gave up trying to persuade Mr. Knight to switch our roles. By three weeks before the opening, Mr. Knight told her to concentrate on Frenchy or he would give the role to someone else. She let up on me too. All I got from her was the back of her head. Every time I saw her she swung around and looked the other way. But I was tired. Tired of all the work, tired of the tension, tired of trying to keep up and always feeling like I was two steps behind where I needed to be.

Destiny had gotten tired too. She was tired of me kissing her goodbye.

Kate babysat Wednesday nights, Teh took Destiny Tuesdays, and Dad said he would have her Saturdays for the afternoon rehearsals, if he was available. The first Saturday he wasn't. I couldn't find anyone except Pete.

"Come on, Pete," I pleaded. "Please."

"I got stuff to do, man," he said.

Stuff that can wait. This can't.

"Please," I almost cried. "I can't miss. What are they going to do if the lead isn't there?"

"When will you be home?"

"Six," I sighed. "I promise."

I didn't want to leave Destiny with Pete. Not if he didn't want to stay with her. I dragged my knapsack out the door and walked up to the school. It was sunny and warm and I wished that I could run back home, pack Destiny in her stroller, and take her to the park. I missed her. I felt an elastic pulling me home, but I pressed forward toward the school.

Mommy's the lead. I'm so sorry.

Every day I was exhausted. My family was exhausted. By the end of practices and rehearsals Uncle Kenny and Auntie Phyllis were taking a turn along with everyone else looking after Destiny.

Grease

Advance tickets on sale for production team only.
Pick up your tickets by Friday April 13.

LIMIT: 6 TICKETS PER TEAM MEMBER

"Dawna," I gasped when I read the notice on the bulletin board. "Six tickets! I need three times that many. My whole darn family is coming."

Right off there was Teh, Dad, Joey, Pete, and Kate. Mrs. Trenton had said Destiny would get in free, but Teh had added up all the rest. We needed twenty-nine tickets. And that was just for the family who said they were coming. As soon as it got around that the tickets were on sale there would be twice that many.

Auntie Mary and Uncle George were coming over from the States, and Richard and his family wanted to come from the mainland. There was Uncle Kenny and Auntie Phyllis and their kids and then Auntie Rachel, who always complained that everyone left her out of everything. If she didn't get a ticket she would never forgive me.

Dawna's family didn't seem to care if they attended or not and were happy to give up their seats. That meant I had twelve tickets. Then Dawna and I asked the other cast members if we could buy their tickets. Most of them didn't have any extra, but by the first dress rehearsal I had thirty-three tickets and thirty-five people who wanted to attend. Joey and Pete said there was no problem—they'd attended every production the school put on and had never bought a ticket yet.

Only the students and staff were allowed to attend the dress rehearsal. By the time Joey dropped me off at the school, the parking lot was full. My head pounded, my nose felt like it would spring a leak any moment, and I could feel huge bags hanging under my eyes. But everyone else was excited.

"Way to go, Jane," I heard someone say as I trudged toward the drama room.

I took a gulp of the orange juice and a bite of the energy

bar Teh had tucked under my arm when I left the house. I began to feel the excitement that filled the school.

I was one of the last to leave the dress rehearsal after the performance.

"You were great, Jane." I turned and Jason pulled me against him.

"You too." I hugged him back, then hung limp in his arms.

He said, "What do you say we go for coffee together when this thing is over?"

"After I die from exhaustion, I'd love to."

By opening night I was ready—on my game. Teh said it was a mixture of adrenaline, stubbornness, great skill, and good medicine. I thought it was because I had no other choice. I had ridden the wave. Now it was cresting and I had to be on top of it.

The lights dimmed. Quiet settled over the crowd on one side of the curtains, and on the other, a hush washed across the actors and dancers.

Mrs. Trenton parted the heavy red velvet curtains. As they folded behind her we heard her say, "Good evening. O'Neil High Junior Musical Theatre Group is delighted that you all came out this evening to watch our production."

Goosebumps appeared on my arms and legs although I was hot and sweaty. My body was alive with a random electrical charge. I could almost hear my blood sizzling through my veins.

"And now a few words from our principal, Mr. Jennings." Her words stacked one on top of the other, muffled behind the beat of my pulse. Drums beating. Pulsing. Beating. Booming.

A young girl fastens deer hooves to her ankles while she listens to the drum. She makes no movement until an earthy guttural song emerges from the centre of the universe.

A thin stream of light broke through backstage. Mrs. Trenton joined us.

"Jane," she whispered. "You're on."

Music filled the theatre, and lights. I saw the stage, the audience beyond, and the heavy curtains disappearing behind the walls. Jane sits on a rock, papier mâché, careful not to sit in the wrong spot or it will collapse. Mark stands in front and off to the side, the place where the audience can see him.

Then the audience disappears, and the papier mâché. My pink dress sprawls across my crinoline. White socks and running shoes, my hair pinned and curled. I am Sandy. Sandy is me. And the stage is home.

Only once again that evening do I see the audience. Only once do I hear anything other than the song and dance and Danny and Kenickie and Frenchy. Only once when I leave the stage, when the music is mixed with a familiar "Mum, Mum, Mum, Mum."

I turn and look back. I squint to allow my eyes to see in the darkness. In front of the first row, Destiny sits in her stroller, waving her hands high in the air, shouting. Behind her in a line are Teh and Dad and Pete and Joey and Kate and Uncle George and Auntie Mary. Behind them in a row are Richard and Auntie Rachel and Auntie Lois and Uncle Curtis and Uncle Kenny and Auntie Phyllis and Auntie Diane, and behind them are cousin Albert and . . .

Author's Note

The Girl with a Baby is a work of fiction, although wholly inspired by the real-life story of my daughter Heather, who gave birth to Yetsa when she was fourteen years old. I am grateful to Heather for her generosity in allowing me to build a fiction around her story. All the characters are my creation, as are the events and relationships.

Since being given the role of mother to a teenage mother and grandmother to a most exquisite granddaughter, I have studied the world of teen parents and believe it is a story we all share. My work with young moms and dads strengthens my conviction that it takes a whole community to raise a child.

Others I would like to thank:

• Tom, for creating a place for me to write this story and for listening each day to my latest sentence or idea.

• Diane Morriss, publisher of Sono Nis Press, for helping me believe I can tell stories and for her constant encouragement and support.

• Laura Peetoom, my gifted editor.

And of course my family for always being there and providing me with ground and air and context and perspective.

About the Author

Sylvia Olsen with her granddaughter Yetsa. —THOMAS KERR, PHOTO

Sylvia Olsen was born and brought up in Victoria, British Columbia. Thirty-one years ago she married into the Tsartlip First Nation, where she has raised her four children. Sylvia works in First Nations community development and specializes in housing and community research. Currently she is conducting an exciting research project, facilitating focus groups with teen parents from the Saanich First Nations in which the teens look at themselves, their babies, and their families, and examine ways the community can provide support to increase the life chances of young parents and their children. As a writer, Sylvia often finds herself writing about the in-between place where First Nations and non-First Nations come together. At this time she is concentrating on writing fiction for young people.

Also by Sylvia Olsen

No Time to Say Goodbye: Children's Stories of Kuper Island Residential School

No Time to Say Goodbye is a fictional account of five children sent to aboriginal boarding school, based on the recollections of a number of Tsartlip First Nations people. These unforgettable children are taken by government agents from Tsartlip Day School to live at Kuper Island Residential School. The five are isolated on the small island, and life becomes regimented by the strict school routine. They experience the pain of homesickness and confusion while trying to adjust to a world completely different from their own. Their lives are no longer organized by fishing, hunting, and family, but by bells, lineups, and chores. In spite of the harsh realities of the residential school, the children find adventure in escape, challenge in competition, and camaraderie with their fellow students.

No Time to Say Goodbye is a story that readers of all ages won't soon forget.

Adopted by the B.C. Teachers' Federation
Nominated for a Saskatchewan Young Readers' Choice Award

ISBN 1-55039-121-6